The Summer of
Sassy Jo

The Summer of Sassy Jo

J. P. Reading

Houghton Mifflin Company
Boston   1989

Library of Congress Cataloging-in-Publication Data

Reading, J. P.
  The summer of Sassy Jo / J. P. Reading.
    p. cm.
  Summary: Almost fourteen. Sara Jo tries to cope with her
conflicting emotions when she goes to spend the summer with her
mother, a reformed alcoholic who abandoned her when she was little.
  ISBN 0-395-48950-4
  [1. Mothers and daughters — Fiction.   2. Family Problems — Fiction.
3. Remarriage — Fiction.]   I. Title.
PZ7.R2353Su   1989   88-34130
[Fic] — dc 19   CIP
                          AC

Printed in the United States of America
P   10 9 8 7 6 5 4 3 2 1

This book is dedicated
to the Age of Mashikian,
and to the man who taught me more about reality
than I ever wanted to know.
For all the years of agony and ecstasy,
and for taking my hand every step of the way,
this one's for you,
Jack Mashikian, my doctor and my friend,
with love.

(And this is also for you Max,
because there hasn't been one day
when you didn't abide with love.)

The Summer of
Sassy Jo

Chapter One

My name is Sara Jo Jacoby, and I have been down here on Long Island, living with my mother, for exactly one week. That means I have exactly twelve more weeks to go.

My mother ran away when I was five and she was an alcoholic. She gave me up to my father, who died last year and left me to his sister, and that's where I live now, officially, in Boston, with my aunt Mimi.

The only reason I'm stuck with Joleen, my mother, for the summer is that Mimi decided she couldn't cope with me anymore, or she wanted to get rid of me for a while anyway. Her words were: "I am no longer able to cope with your behavior, Sara Jo. Since your mother is willing to have you for the summer at least, that's where you're going. You owe her the chance of getting to know you, although how she will manage —" Blah, blah, blah . . . a lot more stuff like "incorrigible" and "how you expect me to put up with," that I didn't bother to listen to.

As far as I was concerned I didn't "owe" my mother one

tiny thing. She was the one who left me when I was five years old, and it wasn't until I was nine that she even remembered she had a daughter. By that time I had forgotten all about her. Or almost, anyway. Harry, my father, had explained the whole thing to me. He said he'd given Joleen about a million chances, but that she preferred drinking and running around to being a wife or a mother.

"Didn't she love me?" I asked him once, when I was a real little kid. "Doesn't she miss me now?"

The only thing he said was, "Your mother doesn't know how to love, Sara Jo. There's something missing inside her."

After he said that I remember I used to go to bed at night and I'd see my mother, sort of swimming up on the ceiling above me, and there would be this big black hole right in the middle of her. I could see her face and her arms and her legs, but where her body should have been, there wasn't anything at all but dark space. That's the part that was missing.

Joleen left right before Christmas. She had taken me to an afternoon performance of *The Nutcracker* ballet, and all during the last act, she was crying and blowing her nose a lot. I couldn't watch the ballet because she was frightening me. So I started to cry too, and when people began turning around, Joleen grabbed my hand and we practically ran out of the theater.

I remember that it was almost dark and there was snow, but it was wet and it wasn't sticking. Sometimes I can still feel that snow on my face and hands. Anyhow, that *Nutcracker* day my mother took me into this dark, grungy bar, where she sat me on a spinning stool and gave me some plastic mixers to play with. We must have been there for hours.

2

I made stick figures out of mixers and drank a lot of Shirley Temples. Finally I fell asleep with my head on the bar. By nine o'clock Joleen decided to pack it in, so she picked me up and pulled me over her shoulders like a papoose, and we galloped into the snow and pranced down the street until a taxi stopped to take us home. I don't remember too much else about that day, but I've heard my father and Aunt Mimi talk about it, so maybe what I know is what I've been told.

The next thing I remember is my mother turning on the lamp near my bed that night and sitting down next to me. I woke up right away, and the first thing I did was try to hide myself in Joleen's lap, as if I were making a nest in her coat. She must have left right after that, because Mimi told me that I woke up the whole house with my screaming, and the doctor had to be called to give me sleeping pills or something.

But that's ancient history. A week ago, Mimi packed me onto the shuttle flight from Boston to New York, and I got my period for the first time somewhere over Rhode Island. I was very nervous, and at first I almost died of embarrassment because I thought I was wetting my pants, only it didn't exactly feel like that. When I stood up I felt something wet and slimy dripping down my leg, and I almost died right there. I had to press my knees together and kind of hobble to the bathroom, where I stuffed my panties with paper towels so that I crunched all the way back to my seat.

It had happened at last. I couldn't believe it. I'd been terrified that there was something the matter with me because I was almost fourteen and everyone else I knew had been moaning about cramps since they were twelve. Once I tried to talk to Mimi about it, but that was a big mistake. First her face

3

got scarlet and then she told me I was a very lucky young lady.

"Why am I lucky?" I asked her. "I don't feel lucky, I feel like a freak!"

"You always dramatize things, Sara Jo," she said. "Don't borrow trouble." And that was the end of our conversation. But I was so concerned that last year I even thought about writing to Joleen and asking her what to do. A moment of insanity on my part.

Joleen Wertzburger. That's my mother's new name. She even invited me to her wedding four years ago, which I thought took a tremendous amount of nerve, and a kind of dumb blindness, too.

The first time I heard from Joleen after she left was on my ninth birthday. She sent me a rag doll with blond wool hair and a card with a note in it that said, "Dear Sassy Jo, I know this is only a very small start, darling, but I hope that you will forgive me and let me make up for all the time I've missed with you. Love, Mommy."

Was she kidding — just like that? No explanations, nothing. She was just planning to move back into my life again.

"She must be going through one of her periods of remorse and rehabilitation," Harry said when I showed him the card. Even that was a lot for him to say because he hated talking about Joleen.

"What does that mean?" I asked him, and then he sat me down and told me some things. Evidently Joleen had written to him a few times since she'd left because she wanted to see me. But Harry wouldn't let her.

"Why not?" I asked.

4

"Because she's not responsible, Sara Jo."

"But if she wanted to see me, if she wrote to you —"

"She wanted to see you so much that she left when you were five, didn't she?" Harry said, and then he went into this big long thing about how Joleen didn't care about anyone but herself, how sick she was. He took the card and ripped it up into little pieces. I remember that night when I was in bed I cried, but the next morning I got rid of the doll she sent me. I wrapped it up in newspaper and then I walked all over the neighborhood looking for the garbage truck. I didn't want to just put it in the trash in our backyard. I didn't want it to be anywhere near me. I wanted it to be gone for good.

Joleen kept trying after that. She wrote to me, and I think she wrote to Harry too. But I wouldn't read her letters, and sometimes weeks would go by and nothing would come from her, so I knew Harry was right. I used to picture her waking up every once in a while with something on her mind, and then she'd remember — oh, yes, that's right, I have a daughter. So she'd sit down and write to me. Who cared?

And then the wedding invitation came. I wouldn't even have opened the envelope, but someone else had addressed it and I didn't recognize the writing. Inside it was a note from her: "Please give us both a new chance, Sara Jo." Like hell I would. I didn't even bother filling in the reply card and sending it back. But about a week before the wedding she called up and I answered the phone.

"Sara Jo?"

"Yes." I didn't know who it was. I didn't even recognize her voice.

"It's me," she said. Really dumb.

5

"Who's 'me'?" But all of a sudden I knew. Something just clicked somewhere and I knew it was Joleen. I wanted to hang up, but I didn't do it. My heart started beating like crazy and for a minute I couldn't even hear what she was saying.

". . . I really wish you'd give me a chance. Just to see you, honey. Would you do that?"

"I'm sorry," I said, "but I'm busy." It was a really jerky thing to say, but she was the one who had come barging through the phone, leaving me totally unprepared.

"Well, if you can't come to the wedding, I know that might be a little strange for you, I only hoped — Do you think you might come and visit us afterwards? Or I could come up there. I'd be glad to do that, Sara Jo." Then, when I didn't say anything she went babbling on. "I'm not drinking now, Sara Jo. I haven't had a drink in two years. I'm not the same person you remember."

"I don't remember anyone," I told her. "I don't remember anything at all." The phone got slippery in my hand because I was perspiring.

"Sara Jo—"

"I have to go now," I said. "Mimi's calling me." And then I did a funny thing. I put the receiver down on the table without hanging it up. I just left it there. Then I walked out of the room and closed the door behind me.

I didn't want to think about Joleen anymore, I decided as the plane hit an air pocket. My stomach dropped down and I felt dizzy. Maybe I was going to faint. Maybe they'd have to carry me off in a stretcher, bleeding . . .

When the pilot finally announced that we were landing at La Guardia, I took out a mirror and looked at my face. All I could see were pasty white cheeks and a curly bush of red hair. The beauty queen cometh for the great reunion scene.

There was a woman waving at me like crazy, and I realized it must be Joleen, with soft brown hair curling around her ears and a wide, perfect smile. Daniel looked dumpy, with a great big nose sitting in the middle of his face.

When Joleen hugged me, I felt a rod go straight up my back, and I let it stay there.

"Sassy Jo, you are so lovely," she said, and I almost gagged. *Sassy Jo?*

She ruffled my hair. "Oh, I guess you don't remember that I used to call you that sometimes."

Did I still look five years old to her?

"This is Daniel," Joleen said, "and that bundle he's holding is Lily — your sister." She sounded awkward. But Mimi had told me about Lily, so I was prepared.

"I'm glad you're here, Sara," the Wertzburger-man said.

"How was your trip?" Joleen asked.

I told her it was okay, and then Daniel gave Lily to Joleen and took my baggage checks. The two of us sat down and stared at each other, and I almost hoped that Lily (whose face I couldn't see) would wake up and create a distraction.

"This is only going to be awkward for a little while, Sara Jo," she seemed to be promising herself more than me. I decided to zing her one.

7

"Do you have any tampons at home? If not I'll have to get some. The curse, right in midair," I said.

"You want — tampons?" She looked surprised.

"Sure. I've been using them for years," I told her airily. What did she know about me?

And tampons were just what she gave me when we got to their home, and I spent a half hour in the bathroom with these crazy directions that started off by saying "Relax!" Oh, sure. I ended up having to make a pad by wrapping Kleenex in toilet paper.

"Come on down," Joleen called up the stairs to me. "Daniel's fixed a surprise for us."

All I wanted to do was lock the door to my room and go to bed. It had been difficult enough trying to make conversation on the way from the airport.

When I went downstairs, only Joleen and Daniel were in the kitchen, and I was relieved that Lily wasn't around. I didn't feel like making baby talk with my two-and-a-half-year-old half sister.

"Come and have some pizza, Sara," Joleen said. She was wearing a cream and lavender robe that looked too young on her. And what was the big deal about pizza?

Joleen explained, "Daniel made it before we came to pick you up. He is known around here as the impresario of pizza." Then she looked at me. "Didn't you want to get changed, Sara? You look so uncomfortable. I thought you'd come down in your nightie." She sounded juvenile. Was it just because she was nervous? Or had all the drinking she'd done drilled holes in her brain? I remembered what my father had said, about something missing inside Joleen. Alcohol eats away brain cells, doesn't it? So maybe she was dealing with only half a deck.

Finally Daniel put the pizza on the table, and Joleen handed me some napkins, but I didn't think I could swallow anything. The sight of oozing mozzarella and runny sauce almost made me gag.

I tried but I couldn't manage more than a few bites. They both kept looking at me, and I felt like some kind of weird specimen under a magnifying glass.

"I'm sorry," I said. "It really looks delicious, but I had a big meal with Mimi right before I left." I hadn't had a thing. I was too nervous to eat.

"That's all right. Don't force yourself, Sassy Jo," Joleen said, and I noticed that her hands were shaking and that she wasn't eating too much either.

"Could you just call me *Sara* Jo? Please?" I knew I sounded angry, but I was trying very hard not to cry. Couldn't they leave me alone? What was I supposed to do — beam away at them as if I'd found an instant family? This little kitchen scene was becoming very uncomfortable.

"All right, Sara Jo," Joleen said quietly.

And then I yawned as hard as I could. "If you don't mind, I'd really like to go to bed now."

"Of course we don't mind," Daniel said, and I stood up.

"Thanks for everything. Good night, Joleen." The minute I said her name, I heard it drop and break on the kitchen tiles, and then there was silence.

" 'Joleen'? I wish you could think of something else to call me, Sara Jo." What did she expect? Mommy dear?

"Yes, ma'am," I said. Then I turned to Daniel. "And good

9

night to you too, sir." That was rotten. What had he done?

In bed I decided that nothing was going to get any better. I wanted to go someplace and lie down dead for the summer. It was awful being on Long Island with Joleen, but it wasn't much good in Boston with Mimi, either. After a while I stuffed a pillow over my face and wondered if I could commit suicide that way, by smothering. Then I lay still with my arms at my sides, and cried myself to sleep, just like a little kid.

How was I going to stand three months of this?

Chapter Two

The next afternoon, when I went up to my room to change into my bathing suit, there was a box of Stayfree Maxi-Pads on my dresser, along with a note from Joleen: "I don't want to step on your toes, Sara Jo, but I really think you'll be more comfortable using these."

Did she know I was lying about the tampons? At that moment I didn't care, I was just so glad to get rid of the tissues and the toilet paper.

When I had gone downstairs that morning, Joleen put an icy glass of orange juice in front of me. I hate orange juice because when I was a little kid they used to stick medicine in it, and the juice had an awful, bitter taste that I never forgot.

"Do you want eggs? Bacon?" She was frying something, with her back to me.

I took a deep breath. "I don't like eggs," I said.

"*Any* eggs?" She turned around, holding a long gleaming fork that looked like a weapon, and I could hear Mimi saying, "Stop being dramatic, Sara Jo."

"I just don't like eggs, period," I told her. "If I eat eggs, I throw up."

"That's funny. Mimi didn't tell me you still didn't like them. I thought you'd outgrown that by now."

"Mimi! Why would Mimi tell you anything?" I had a creepy feeling.

Joleen sat down near me. "Because I'm your mother, Sara Jo, and there isn't anything about you that I don't want to know."

Oh yeah? Since when?

Any minute, I thought, the weepy music will come up. She probably has the violins waiting on the back porch. What did she expect me to do? Fall into her arms and thank her for being so worried about me for my whole life? By this time I was pretty miserable.

Joleen reminded me of one of those little capsules kids buy in the five and ten. They come in all colors, and the instructions are that you put one of them in water and in a couple of minutes it grows into this great big animal, or whatever it's supposed to be, usually a dinosaur or something. That's how she acted, like she was a little pink pill that had just popped itself into a gallon of water, and presto! Instant mother!

"Am I supposed to get all choked up because you've been so concerned about me for all these years?" I asked her meanly. "There's not one tiny thing about me that doesn't matter to you, I suppose."

She had been folding and refolding her napkin, and for one scary moment I thought she was going to cry, but she didn't. She looked up and stared straight at me.

"That's right, Sara," she said quietly. "Now how about if I fry you some bacon? You and I have a lot to talk about, but I don't think we have to do it all in one morning. I don't want to push you, and I don't mean to rush things. If you want to know, I'm a little nervous myself." She laughed shakily.

But she was so intense that she frightened me. Maybe Joleen knew all kinds of things about me that were none of her business. Maybe for all those years when I'd been ignoring that she was even alive Mimi had been feeding her all these little bits and pieces of me, and I never knew. Although I wasn't so crazy about my aunt Mimi, I never thought she'd be a traitor, especially when she knew perfectly well how my father and I felt on the subject of Joleen. Maybe there wasn't anybody in the world left to trust.

"Sara Jo, are you all right?" Joleen put a plate of toast and bacon down in front of me.

"I'm never all right," I said. "I'm very strange."

"I bet you're not all that strange," she said, sitting down near me with a cup of coffee. Then I watched her take a deep breath, as if she had something important to say, and I got scared again. In my family — with Mimi and Harry — nobody said things straight out at you. If I did something wrong I was punished or something, but we never had great discussions about it. My father could speak hundreds of words with just one nasty look, and the one thing he hated was long, boring explanations about why I had done this or that, or how I felt about things. And with Mimi it was even worse. I swear sometimes she used to look at me like I was an alien. But Joleen gave me the feeling that nothing was going to be too small for us to talk about, that there wasn't anything about me she wouldn't like to explore in depth. Well, she was in for a big surprise because I wasn't going to give.

"Are we about to have our first mother-daughter talk?" I asked before she could open her mouth to say anything.

She looked startled. "How about just a regular talk? Between two people — you and me?"

I shrugged. "So talk if you want to," I said, crunching down on a piece of bacon.

Good old Joleen. She zeroed right in and took my appetite away.

"You've been having a hard time, haven't you," she said, "since your father died?"

"I'm always having a hard time," I said. "According to Mimi, I make everything difficult for myself."

"And is that true?"

"How do I know?" I pushed my plate away. I didn't want to look at her, but I could feel her eyes on me, as if she had me pinned down as flat as a dead butterfly.

"Do you have a lot of friends, Sara Jo?" Her voice was gentle, but she wasn't fooling me. Miss Information Please was trying to scalp me for all the pertinent data she could get.

"No," I said, "I don't have a lot of friends."

I used to have a few friends, kids I really liked, but I didn't have to tell her that. If I did, she'd want to know why I didn't still have them, and then what would I say? Because they all started going nutty over boys, and I didn't have anything to talk to them about anymore? And because they were into trying all these crazy things, and I was afraid? The one time I'd even tried taking a few puffs of grass with some kids, Mimi had smelled it, and she came barging into my room, screaming at us and sending everyone home as if we were all little kids. And then she'd called up all their mothers . . . it was awful. I couldn't even stand remembering it.

"I know someone who might be a friend for you," Joleen was saying, "if you're interested."

"Thanks, but I'm not." I knew I was really being terrible, but I didn't know how to stop.

"Look, you're going to have a very boring summer if you plan to just sit around this house being gloomy." She sighed. "Try to make just a little effort with me, will you, Sara? I know this isn't easy for either one of us." When I didn't answer, she went right on talking. "The people next door have a daughter. Her name is Katie. Katie Delaney. She's a little younger than you, but —"

"So?"

"So we thought maybe you'd like to go over there and meet her."

It wasn't a question, but I answered anyway.

"No, I would not like to," I said.

"Well, please go and do it anyhow." Joleen was finally losing her patience with me. Not that I could really blame her. I was definitely on a bad roll. "It's the house to the left of us, and they have a pool," she added.

"Big deal," I said, but I knew I was going to have to go over, or Joleen would probably freeze me out, the way Mimi sometimes did, and I wasn't looking forward to living in total silence for the next three months. I'd had enough of that in Boston. I knew I should make some kind of effort with Joleen too, but I didn't know how or what to do.

15

"Look at it this way. It will be better than just being with me and Daniel all summer," she said.

"What about Lily? Where's Lily?" I asked, to change the subject.

"She's taking a nap. She always does after breakfast. You'll meet her awake soon."

Oh good.

"She'll be up by the time you're back from the Delaneys."

It was obvious that I was stuck. "I'll go now," I told her. I mean, if you knew you were going to have your tooth pulled without novocaine, you wouldn't want to think about it for a couple of hours first, would you?

A few moments later I was walking up the Delaneys' driveway, nervous about meeting Katie and wanting to hide out in my room and read. Maybe no one will be home, I thought as I pushed the bell. No such luck. There was Katie, staring out at me through the screen, with the tip of one long pigtail stuck in her mouth.

"Hi," I said. "You're Katie, right? I'm Sara Jo Jacoby. I'm staying next door."

"Hi." That was all. Katie seemed to have a limited vocabulary. She pulled some more braid into her mouth, and the two of us just hung there like dopes.

"Oh, hey, you want to see our pool?" She seemed to remember that I was still there. "Your mother said that I should show it to you." She pushed the door open, and when she came outside, I saw that the screen had made a waffle pattern on her forehead.

"How come you're not wearing any shoes?" Katie asked,

and I noticed her sandals just as she started screaming, "Look out! You have a worm stuck on your foot!"

I looked down and there was a fuzzy green caterpillar inching across my toes. "So?"

"So get it off you! Step on it or something! I hate crawling things!"

I sat down and gently lifted the caterpillar from my ankle and put it on the grass. There was no way I could kill anything. I even walked around those little brown ants that build their homes between cracks on the sidewalk.

"Mission accomplished," I said, getting up.

Katie put her hands on her hips and looked at me. "Do you want to see the pool, or not?"

"Sure," I told her. "I always think about Esther Williams when I see a pool. I've seen all her old movies on television. Could that lady swim." I was just trying to make conversation, but Katie gave me a dumb look.

"Esther Williams? Who's Esther Williams?" She was unlatching the back gate. "We only have educational television in our house."

Well, la-di-da, I thought. We had cable, and I used to watch anything I wanted to when Mimi wasn't home. So far, my entire sex education was a product of TV flicks. Or it was until my aunt got home early one day from her weekly bridge luncheon. I was stretched out on the floor of the den with the curtains drawn so the room would be nice and dark, watching this porn flick and wondering if people actually did things like that in real life. Mimi took one look and flew into little pieces. According to her the movie was filthy and disgusting and anyone who could watch such a piece of trash had to be seriously disturbed. She had the cable disconnected the next day, and it was a week before she said more to me than "Please pass the salt."

Then I saw the pool. Esther Williams would have died. It was an enormous white-tile paradise. But that's not all. The water was a deep indigo blue! I couldn't believe it.

"Oh, Katie," I said. I wanted to tell her I'd be her best friend for the rest of our lives if she'd just give me pool privileges every day.

"Yeah, it's pretty nice," Katie said, but she wasn't looking at the pool, she was looking down at her feet. "I wish I could go barefoot," she said.

"Why can't you?"

"Because my mother says you get infections," Katie said. The poor kid. Can't watch TV. Can't go barefoot. And I bet there were a lot of other things Katie wasn't allowed to do either. I could sympathize with her.

"Could we sit here on the side, and hang our feet in the water?" I asked hopefully.

Katie frowned. "No one is allowed in the pool until they've showered. That's a Delaney, and there are no exceptions," she said emphatically.

"What's a Delaney?"

"A Delaney is a rule of the house, to be obeyed by members of the household, family, and friends," she told me seriously.

"My aunt Mimi would love them. She adores rules."

"Who's your aunt Mimi?"

"I live with her in Boston. She's my dead father's sister."

18

"Oh. I thought Mrs. Wertzburger was your mother and that you were coming here to live." She looked over at Joleen's house as if someone had been lying to her, and I saw the pool floating out from under me.

"She *is* my mother. She abandoned me, but that doesn't mean she's not my mother. It just means that I don't know her very well, that's all. But I am going to be here for the summer."

"Abandoned?" Katie's glasses slid off her nose and she pushed them back up.

"Well, it was like being abandoned. I haven't seen Joleen since I was practically an infant."

Katie was all excited. "Did she leave you on a *door*step, or something?"

"Katie, I was five!"

"Well, how was I supposed to know?" She sounded disappointed. "So where did she leave you, then?"

"She *left* me with my father, that's where," I told her, looking down at the pool and wanting just to jump in, despite all the Delaneys. And then I had this horrifying thought: what if I wasn't supposed to go swimming while I had my period?

"So what did your father do?" Katie was insatiable.

"He died. I just told you." It had gotten much hotter, and little black flies were biting me. I decided that if Katie wasn't going to invite me to use the pool, then it was time for me to leave.

"I'm going to go," I told her. "Thanks for showing me your pool." Right then I didn't care much about swimming anyhow. Katie was just a kid. It would be a bore having to put up with her questions every day. Besides, I didn't know what to do about my period.

"Where are you going?" She really looked upset. I noticed that she bit her nails — way down. My father told me that if you bite your nails, you have a lot of unresolved problems, and Mimi said the same thing.

"Don't you want to go swimming?" she asked.

"Sure, I guess so." It was too much to resist.

"So get your bathing suit then, and don't forget to take a shower," Katie warned.

I put my hand up. "Delaney number six thousand one hundred and three! I shall obey," I said and gave her a short salute.

Back in my room, I started to line the inside of my bathing suit with Maxi-Pads. They have these adhesive strips down the backs of them, but I didn't know if those were waterproof or not. I slumped down on the bed, wondering what to do. How did I get to be this age and know so little? Joleen would know. Damn! I'd heard her cooing around in Lily's room when I passed by. But I certainly wasn't going to let her know that I couldn't figure out a couple of simple things for myself.

Come to think of it, I didn't really know anything about my period. I was totally uninitiated; my body had hardly begun to change. I mean, I still wear these dumb undershirts with bows on them! And you can see the bow right through my blouses and sweaters because it makes this lump . . .

I started to perspire. Ask Joleen, or not?

I decided definitely no. And then I remembered that about a year ago Mimi had given me this nerdy little booklet. It had a blue cover with a white calling card on it, and written on the card was "Personally Yours," in this fancy handwriting. I'd known right away what it was. We'd had all that stuff in seventh-grade hygiene anyhow, but I'd never paid much attention. Actually, I was as embarrassed as Mimi when she gave the booklet to me. Some things you just didn't talk about in a private family like mine. No doubling up in the bathroom, or anything like that. Even when I was a little kid.

Now I was desperately trying to remember if "Personally Yours" had anything about swimming in it. But all I could see were these drawings of eggs and sperm shooting around inside of this V. That's what's the matter with books like that, they never tell you the stuff you really want to know. They fill your head up with all of this biological junk when all you wanted were a few practical, everyday tips.

Finally I decided that I'd brave it. The fearless Sara Jo puts on her padded swimsuit and prepares to rival Esther Williams. Then I looked in the mirror. Not terrific, but I wasn't really lumpy. Not if you didn't look too closely.

Katie frowned when she saw me, but I pretended not to notice and slid one foot into the water.

"No!" Katie screamed.

"What's the matter?" What was wrong? Was she giving the family barracuda some exercise? But then I got the message.

"A Delaney, right?" I said.

She nodded and looked up at me, blinking back the sun. She looked like a little kid in her blue plaid bathing suit.

"Katie, how old are you?"

"Going on eleven. Why?"

Ten! I was practically her baby-sitter!

"Nothing," I said, sitting down next to her. "What's the Delaney that says I can't swim?"

"Your hair," she told me. "You can't let the drain get all gopped up," and she pointed to a white rubber cap looped over her wrist. "You need to have one of these."

And where was I supposed to get one of these? I was sure that I couldn't borrow Mrs. Delaney's. She'd probably be afraid of bugs, or lice.

"I don't have one," I told Katie, who really looked surprised. Did she think I carried bathing caps around with me, just in case?

"Wait!" She ran toward the garage, and when she came running back she had something that looked like a giant sunflower dangling from her hand. Oh no. Was I going to have to wear that thing on my head?

Katie held the cap out to me. "It belonged to my grandmother, but she died."

Her grandmother? I pulled the cap on and snapped it under my chin.

"Do I pass Delaney inspection?" I asked her, and when she nodded I dove in from the side of the pool. Then I surfaced and floated on my back. It was terrific, with the sun directly above me, burning down on my face.

"Hey, Sassy Jo, are you going to live in that pool, or what?" Katie called to me.

I turned over and swam to where she was sitting. "Katie, I know you heard that name from Joleen, but it's not funny, so please don't ever use it again, okay?"

"Sure, okay. I'm sorry." Katie looked upset.

"All right, but don't forget," I said, warning her.

When I finally came out of the water, I remembered the pads right away because I felt as if I were carrying around a load of wet diapers. Luckily nothing seemed to be trailing out of my suit, and when I looked over my shoulder, I was relieved to see that the pool was still indigo. Maybe the cold water had stopped my period. It was a happy thought.

"Hey, you want to play water polo?" Katie said. "It's really fun if you want to try."

"Hi, girls." Joleen was coming toward us, wearing a T-shirt and shorts, and Lily was tagging after her.

"Say hi to Sara Jo," Joleen said, but Lily just hid her head behind her mother's leg. And that was totally all right with me. Lily was part of the Wertzburger house, and so I had to accept her, but our "relationship" didn't have to go any further than that.

"She's shy at first," Joleen explained. "Sara, where did you ever get that?" She poked her finger at my sunflower cap and laughed.

"From Katie's dead grandmother," I said. "She refused her right to be buried in it."

Katie was giggling, and Joleen laughed, too.

"It's good to see you have a sense of humor, Sara," Joleen said. She was giving me this great big smile, and I just couldn't stand it because she was rushing, trying to gather me in too fast. Presto, a new family for Sara Jo, including a brand-new father.

Well, I had to admit Daniel seemed pretty nice — maybe it wouldn't be so bad if I really were his daughter, but I

23

wasn't. Not that Harry and I were close — which might be the understatement of the year — but Harry was what I had. I belonged to Harry, and Daniel already had Lily. Right. I also had a baby half sister, and a woman who wanted to be my mother again. I just couldn't accept it; maybe I never would.

"Thanks for the pool, Katie. It was super," I said, and then I ran toward the back gate, feeling like I was escaping, and hoping that all my Maxies would stay in place.

Chapter Three

I didn't see much of the Wertzburgers at all for the next few days. It was weird living in a house with three strangers. There was this happy little family, and then there was me. And the worst part of everything was that Joleen kept trying so hard. I felt cornered every time I was alone with her. She always wanted to talk, to find out everything she could about me. No one had ever done that before, so I suppose I should have felt flattered or something, but I didn't. All I wanted to do was run away from her. "How do you feel about . . . ?" "Do you like to . . . ?" "Why don't you . . . ?" Endless questions and suggestions, until I felt as if she were peeling off layers of my skin, trying to dissect every piece of me to find the real Sara Jo hiding somewhere inside. She made me feel like curling up into a ball so I could protect myself.

I was spending most of my time in Katie's pool. I felt free and light in the water. No one could get to me there. Sometimes I played water polo with Katie, and sometimes I practiced my diving, but mostly I was just there by myself, traveling in fantasies where I was a mermaid, plunging into the depths of the ocean, discovering hidden treasures.

I finally met Katie's mother. Clovis. That's her name. Imagine holding a newborn baby in your arms and saying, "This is Clovis." She's a very twitchy lady and she has this thick black hair that hangs down almost to her waist.

When I first met her, Clovis said, "How nice that Katie has another little girl to play with this summer. All her other little friends have gone away to camp."

Why was Clovis calling me "little"? I was almost old enough to be Katie's godmother. Katie was a cute kid, but we were definitely in different leagues.

"Why didn't you go to camp, too?" I asked her after Clovis had gone inside.

"I can't go to camp because I'm allergic," Katie said, bouncing around on the diving board.

"What are you allergic to?" I asked her.

"Pollen, ragweed, dandelions, hollyhocks — practically everything. I break out in these prickly red and white clumps —"

"Why don't you have them now?"

"Because I take shots and stuff all summer. The doctor says maybe I'll grow out of it, but by that time I'll probably be too old for camp," she said matter-of-factly.

Just then a fuzzy yellow jacket came buzzing around us, and Katie did a backflip into the pool.

"What's the matter?" I yelled down to her.

"Is the bee gone?"

I looked around. "I don't see it."

"I'm allergic to bees, too," she said. "If I get stung and

don't have a shot in a couple of seconds, I could drop down dead."

I grinned. Katie could be pretty dramatic.

One way or another, I was managing to keep out of Joleen's way. And Daniel's too, but that was only because he was an obstetrician, and he was always being called to the hospital at crazy hours.

One afternoon Joleen enticed me by making chocolate sodas, and we were sitting out in the back of the house drinking them. I wondered if Joleen really wished she were having Scotch instead. I didn't understand much about her drinking thing, but once, a long time ago, Harry had told me she was an alcoholic.

"What's that?" I asked him.

"A person who can't control her drinking, who would rather drink than do anything else," he said.

"Drink what?" I was confused.

But he just shook his head and refused to answer.

"Don't ask so many questions. You're too young to understand any of this, Sara Jo."

But I wasn't too young to go to the library, where I read a lot of stuff I really couldn't understand about alcoholics. The one thing I did get is that they had a disease, and that disease usually messed up their lives, and everybody else's too. Well, that was Joleen all right. She must have preferred booze to being with Harry and me. I used to picture her sometimes, off in some cruddy little room with nothing in it but bottles of liquor. There'd be a little space in the center of the room (which my imagination also supplied with rats and spiders) and she'd be sitting there all day long, just swilling away. I even used to have dreams about it.

That day Lily was in bed for her nap, and I sat around with Joleen, drinking my soda for about half an hour. The two of us were talking about me again when I made a sudden decision.

"I wanted to ask you some things about my period," I said, and I could hear my voice shake. I knew she wouldn't know it, but I realized I was about to make this big effort and let her in a little. Maybe I just wanted to see what it would feel like.

"Sure." Joleen sounded relaxed. "What about it?"

"I was just wondering . . . I couldn't remember if it was all right for me to go swimming. I mean I never had much opportunity before, and I already did, but —"

"Oh, Sara Jo, can you imagine all the Delaneys you'd get if they knew?"

"You know about Delaneys?" I asked her, and we both started to laugh.

"Do I know about them? Sara, I think the *world* knows a Delaney when it hears one. And the world obeys!" And then she stopped laughing. "Oh, I shouldn't mock. They're very good people. Anyhow, we were talking about the curse when you go swimming, right?"

"Right."

"Sara, I think I'd better tell you something first," Joleen looked at me seriously, and I started to get nervous. She had gotten that look again. She was beaming in on me.

"What?" I asked her.

"I called Mimi the other night. It was right after you'd gone to bed," she said.

"So what?"

"Well, I happened to mention that you had your period —"

"*Happened* to mention?" I sat up straight. I couldn't believe it!

"Yes, that's right, I happened to, and then —"

"Oh, sure," I cut her off. " 'Hi, Mimi, this is Joleen Wertzburger. How are things? Oh, by the way, Sara Jo got her period. I know it's a disgusting subject, but —' "

"There's nothing *disgusting* about it." She looked surprised. "You can believe this or not, Sara Jo, but I only mentioned it to Mimi because I didn't know that this was the first time for you, but Mimi said — well, I guess you know what she said. I'm sorry, honey, but when you asked me for tampons, I thought you knew what it was all about." Joleen was being so gentle that I couldn't stand it.

"I *do* know what it's all about, except for one or two things like swimming," I told her.

"Okay. What about swimming?" she asked.

"Can I do it?"

"Sure, you can swim, but you might want to experiment with some junior tampons. You'd be more comfortable with them, probably," Joleen said.

Great. It would probably take me the rest of the summer to figure out how to use them.

"Listen, babe," Joleen said reassuringly, "we'll figure it out the next time. You're about over it now, aren't you?"

I nodded.

Honey. Babe. I wish she'd stop talking like that. I didn't want to be called those names. They embarrassed me.

"Okay, Sara, what else?"

"Nothing else. No big deal. I was just curious." I'd said enough personal things for one day.

"All right. Now how about if we go shopping tomorrow?"

I knew Joleen was really trying hard, so even though I didn't want to go, I told her I would.

The next morning Joleen and I backed out of the driveway in her new car. It was a shiny black Corvette with wire wheels. Exactly the kind of car I'd like to own in a few years. I could just picture myself cruising along the Charles River in Boston with the top down.

Daniel told me that everyone on Long Island drove at least one car. It was called "having wheels," and unless you had them, you stayed in your house and watched the crabgrass spread.

We drove to a shopping mall that had canned music piped in, and huge tubs of gardenia trees growing all over the place.

"Saks Fifth Avenue." Joleen grinned. "Fancy enough, Sara Jo?"

"Sure." Fancy made me nervous.

"Oh, Sara, look at this!" Joleen was holding up a white silk nightshirt with lace panels down the sides.

"It's nice," I said, but I was embarrassed. Obviously she wanted to get it so she'd look pretty for Daniel, and thinking about that made me uncomfortable.

We wandered through the department.

"I thought you might like a few new bras." When Joleen said that, I could feel the heat spreading up from my neck. *New* bras? *New* ones?

She was holding out a lavender bra and looking at it critically. "Do you have anything this color? It's kind of pretty."

"Maybe just . . . a white one?" I could hear my voice shaking. What was I talking about? What did I think I could fill up a bra with, except maybe tissue paper.

Joleen shook her head. "Absolutely not. Around here everything is color-coordinated. Look at all these suburban mamas, Sara Jo. I bet their bras and panties match their pants suits. It would definitely be tacky just sticking to white. Trust me."

In a few minutes she had filled my arms with narrow strips of nylon in rainbow colors.

All the way to the dressing rooms, I prayed that Joleen wouldn't come in with me. I had these ratty old cotton panties on, and I hadn't even worn an undershirt because it was so hot.

"Sara Jo, why don't you try some of these on and I'll go back and see what else I can find."

I raced out of my clothes and pulled on a pair of peach-colored bikinis and a matching bra. Don't let her come back. Oh, please don't let her come back and see me.

My hands were shaking so much that it took me forever to get the bra fastened, and when I finally did I was afraid to look at myself in the mirror. Instead I looked down, expecting to see a lot of bunched and puckered nylon with no skin to fill it out. But it wasn't true! There I was looking at

31

myself, perfectly filling up a double-A bra. I was ecstatic. I'd never have to wear another undershirt again!

"Sara, where are you?"

"In here." I waved a hand outside the curtains.

"How's it going?" she called.

"Fine, I'll be right out."

"The sizes okay?" she asked.

"Perfect," I draped the underwear over my arms and came out.

"Next stop, tank tops and shorts," Joleen said, "You'll suffocate in those jeans all summer."

When we got home I carried everything upstairs and Joleen went next door to get Lily. Then, because the house was quiet, and I was all alone, I decided to take my time, and try some things on and really look at myself.

I pulled a royal blue bra and matching panties from the pile on my bed. Then I looked into the full mirror on the closet door. Wow. I looked good, I really did. My breasts were small, but if I cupped my hands under them, I looked almost busty. I had a nice flat stomach, and the rest of me wasn't so bad either. I got this crazy idea. I stripped off the bikinis and bra and just stood looking at myself. I'd never done anything like that before. In my house modesty was second only to virginity. Aunt Mimi had even taught me how to get into my nightgown without ever being down to my skin, and you practically have to be a contortionist to manage that.

I stood in front of the mirror and looked at myself, front, back, and profile. I stared for so long that I got goose bumps, and I finally had to get dressed.

*

"Hey, Sara Jo, you want to come over and fry some marshmallows with me?" Katie was squeaking the kitchen door back and forth.

"Quit that and come in," I told her. She'd been peering through the screen and getting her waffle marks back. "How do you fry marshmallows?"

"Well, we have this grill that has a metal sheet you can pull over the coals, and when it gets real hot, you start rolling —"

"Rolling?"

"Yeah, rolling. You roll the marshmallows around real fast so they don't stick, and then you have fried marshmallows. You want to try?" Katie was almost salivating.

"Well . . ." I didn't have any other plans.

"Sara Jo," Joleen called, "if you're anywhere in the house, please don't leave."

"In the kitchen," I called, making a face at Katie.

"Come on, sweetheart," Joleen was saying to Lily as they came down the hall.

"Hi, Katie. Say hello to Katie, Lily."

"Katie give lollipops?" she asked, stretching a sticky little hand out and grabbing the ruffle on Katie's bathing suit.

Katie shook her head. "I don't have any," she said, showing Lily her empty hands.

"Please." Lily looked like an orphan.

"Tomorrow," Katie promised, "okay?"

"Sara," Joleen said, "I have a huge favor to ask you."

She sure did, because I knew what it was going to be.

"The baby-sitter didn't show," Joleen said, "and Clovis is

33

out. Believe me, Sara, I don't like cutting in on your time, but it's the last minute, and I don't have any choice. Will you watch Lily for a few hours?"

"All right," I agreed, a little grudgingly.

"Great," Joleen said, "I have to rush, but no pool, huh?"

"No pool."

Joleen picked up Lily and kissed her on both cheeks, the forehead, and the lips. "Mama will be back before you sneeze, baby," she said.

"Lily like?"

"No. Lily won't like too much, but it'll be okay," and Joleen made a crazy face until she got Lily to laugh. "Be good," she said, grabbing her car keys and dashing out the back door.

After she left, I wondered if she'd remembered that Lily didn't even like me. Every time I came near her she scrunched her face up like she was going to cry. Joleen's car wasn't even down the driveway before she started in, but she only got worse when I picked her up.

"I'll take her," Katie said, "she'll stop in a while. She always does this as soon as your mom leaves, but she gets over it, don't you Lily-Lily?"

"Mrs. Wertzburger, you mean," I told Katie.

"Huh?" her mouth dropped open. "But she *is* your mom?"

"The jury is still out on that one."

Katie looked confused, and she stopped bouncing Lily. "I guess we can't fry marshmallows today, huh?"

"Not with the pool so close to the marshmallows," I said.

"What else could we do?" Katie asked.

"Wait a minute. I've got an idea," I told her. "I'll be right back," and I ran into the living room for *TV Guide*.

"We're in luck," I told Katie, flipping through the pages. "There's an afternoon horror flick on. Hey, it's a classic —"

"I don't want to watch," Katie said, doodling Lily around on her lap.

"What do you mean you don't want to watch? Are you kidding? It's *Dracula*, Katie. The original *Dracula*! I'll make popcorn and —"

"Monsters scare me. I can't help it."

"But this isn't a monster. It's a vampire. He only sucks blood." But Katie still looked frightened. "Don't worry, we're going to watch together, remember?"

"Well —"

"You're going to love it, Katie," I promised, picking Lily up and putting her in her jump seat.

"Out!" she shouted. "Out, now!"

"If you shut up, Lily, I'll give you some popcorn to eat and let you watch television with Katie and me. *Kemo sabe*, white man?" Lily loved playing Indian princess. She even had a pair of beaded moccasins and a necklace made out of feathers.

I got out a large pot and some oil, and Katie and I made mountains of buttery popcorn. We settled around the TV with Lily lying on her stomach, licking each piece thoroughly before she put it in her mouth. Then the credits came on, and I didn't take my eyes off the screen.

I even gave up on Katie. Every time I looked at her, she had her fingers spread across her face.

When I checked Lily during a commercial, she was asleep, with one finger poked in her ear, and her small bowl of popcorn was practically full.

For about an hour, I didn't see anything but the tube. And then I heard Katie snoring next to me. I just couldn't believe it.

And Lily was — where was Lily?

First I just calmly started calling her name, and then I was yelling all over the house for her. Katie woke up looking frightened, and she started searching, too.

Lily wouldn't go upstairs. She never went up unless one of us was with her, because she hated it up there. That's where she had to do all the things she didn't like doing, like taking naps and baths, and going to bed alone in the dark.

We looked under chairs and tables. We checked every closet, beating at the clothes while we screamed, "Lily, Lily, Lily," over and over again. And all the time I knew she wasn't going to answer. I knew it.

It was Katie who saw the front door first. It was open, and the storm door was off the latch.

"Katie, you go look outside, okay? And you'd better tell your mother if she's home. Maybe she'll think of something . . ."

I didn't want Katie to leave, and I didn't want Clovis Delaney coming over and poking around, but I had to do something. I was terrified.

I sat down on the couch in the living room. I wanted just to listen, because Katie and I had been screaming so much. What if Lily had tried to answer, and we couldn't hear her?

I tried to think, but I was too scrambled. After a few moments I jumped up and started running around again. This time I looked in the dishwasher and the oven — nothing.

Finally, I did look upstairs. Even though I knew Lily wasn't going to be there, I had to do something.

No Lily on the potty. No Lily in the crib. No Lily on the king-sized Wertzburger bed. Then — there she was, sitting on the floor in my room, singing to herself. That morning I'd let her finger-paint in there while Joleen was taking a shower, and now she had her paints spread out all around her, and she was busy mucking up all my new panties and bras with every color she could get her grubby little fingers into.

Never mind that I leave my clothes all over the place, I was so mad that I didn't even feel relieved that she wasn't dead. I was furious! I ran over, pushed the underwear away from her and slapped her hand. Naturally, she started to cry.

"You can yell your brains out, I don't care. Look what you did! Do you see what you've done?" I picked her up, but then I didn't know what to do with her.

"Lily, shut up." I shook her. "You're a real rotten little kid, do you know that?" And that was when Lily started throwing up. Pieces of popcorn and goo. Just what I needed. I shifted her under my arm and carried her down the hall to the bathroom. She was crying and coughing so much that I started to feel sorry for her. I was also a little guilty for not picking up my stuff.

Then I swung around to get her through the bathroom door, and Lily's head crashed into the doorjamb. "Lily?" But suddenly she wasn't Lily anymore. She was like a sack of oranges. I almost dropped her. "Lily? *Lily!*" I held her up in front of me and she sagged like a rag doll.

I wasn't shaking. In fact, I was calm. I carried Lily back to my room and laid her down on the bed.

The next thing I knew, Clovis and Katie were there. I couldn't hear what they were saying because there was this loud buzzing in my ears, as if my head were stuck in a wasps' nest, and it wouldn't clear up, even when I banged my hands against my ears.

I kept looking at Lily, and waiting for her to move. But she was as still as stone, and I was sure she was dead. Clovis went over to kneel by the bed and take her hand, and Katie was crying.

My ears cleared up when I heard the sirens, and then two men were in the room, carrying a stretcher between them. When they lifted Lily onto it, she looked so tiny. Had I really killed her? I wished they wouldn't take her away from the house.

Clovis had her arm around me and I had to try hard not to push her away. I just wanted to be left alone.

"Sara?"

Go away.

"Sara?" She shook me, just the way I'd done to Lily.

"What is it, Mrs. Delaney?" I stared at her without seeing her.

"I want you to be a good girl and go with my Katie to our house, and I'll go to the hospital with Lily. But before we leave, I have to ask you one question. These men need to know what happened to Lily. Do you know why she's unconscious, dear?"

"I threw her against the wall," I said. I wanted to cry. What did she think had happened?

"Sara!"

Then I looked at her and I felt sorry. "She banged her head while I was carrying her into the bathroom. I was mad because she'd messed up —"

"That's all right, Sara Jo. That's all right." She tap-tapped my shoulder.

What was all right?

Katie pinched my elbow. "Come on, Sara Jo, we have to go. Didn't you hear my mother?"

"Are we following Delaney Seven Hundred and Forty-nine — Proper Manners at a Funeral?" I started to laugh, but I couldn't.

"Don't say that, Sara. Lily isn't dead. My mother just said so."

Katie held my hand while we walked over to her house, as if she were afraid I was either going to run away, or fall down. Or maybe she did it to make me feel better.

She led the way to their cellar, which was supposed to be a rumpus room, with a dart board, a Ping-Pong table, and Lucite chairs. Definitely from the school of ugly.

"What really happened, Sara Jo?" Katie asked me. Her glasses were sliding all over her nose again.

"What do you mean, 'What really happened?'? What the hell do you *think* happened? Do you think I tried to kill her?"

"No!" Katie jumped up. "Do you want a soda?"

"Okay," I said.

Katie and I drank cherry soda, but we didn't have very

much to say to each other. I thought I should call the hospital, only I didn't know which hospital, and I didn't want to ask Katie. I was afraid to find out.

"Are you hungry, Sara Jo? We have some chocolates. I don't think they're too stale."

I heard the click of a door upstairs and stood up, but then I didn't move. It was as if I were playing Statues. If I didn't move, if I didn't breathe, maybe Lily would still be alive.

A stair creaked, and then Daniel was there, and I ran into his arms and put my head against his chest. Daniel rubbed my back, and as I stood there, safe against him, I knew Lily was dead.

"Sara Jo?" He held me away from him. "Are you all right?"

I nodded, but my chin was trembling.

"Where's Joleen?" I asked, although I didn't want to see her. I didn't ever want to have to face Joleen again.

"She's still at the hospital."

Why? I wondered. And then I thought that maybe she was waiting until Daniel could get me packed and to the airport, so she wouldn't have to see me again either.

"Are you ready, Sara?" Daniel asked me.

"Where are you taking me?" I said.

"I'm taking you back to our house, honey. Isn't that all right?"

And then I suddenly realized that Lily must be alive. Daniel was smiling, and we were just going back next door.

"Lily has a mild concussion, and they want to watch her for a day or two, just to be safe. But it's not serious."

Suddenly, I had to tell Daniel everything that had happened. So I did. I even told him how angry I'd gotten at Lily.

But he wasn't mad. He just put his arm around me and let me talk.

Joleen came in a few minutes after we'd made some fresh iced tea. I wanted to die. I couldn't even look at her.

"Sara Jo?"

"Hi." But I still didn't look. Not that it really mattered. As far as I was concerned, Joleen only had one real daughter, and she was lying in a little hospital bed.

"Sara Jo, please look at me." Her voice sounded tinny, as if it were coming from far away.

Finally I did look at her. She didn't have any makeup on, and she looked tired. A memory came back to me: that's how she looked when she had a hangover. Even when I was a kid I knew what a hangover was like, although I didn't know what it actually was. I remembered Joleen being in bed while Mimi sent me up with a pot of tea, and told me to come right back downstairs because my mother felt ill that morning. When I was little, I always thought Joleen was dying. Lots of times I'd open her door a crack to listen, just to see if she were still breathing.

"I want you to tell me what happened. And whatever it was, we'll work it out. Are you listening to me, Sara Jo?"

"Sure."

"Well?"

"I'm sorry," I said stiffly. "Lily threw up, and I was carrying her to the bathroom to wash her off. And then — I'm not even sure how it happened, but her head banged into the door."

"Was she crying?"

"Yes. That's probably why she threw up."

41

"Why was she crying, Sara?" Joleen's voice had gotten whispery, and it gave me the creeps. I thought, maybe she really thinks I tried to kill Lily.

"She was crying because I yelled at her and I slapped her hand for getting finger paints all over my new underwear, that's why."

"She *what*?? Is that all she did? She's a baby, Sara Jo! She was just playing. Didn't you stop to think it would all wash out?" Joleen was letting her mask slip, and beneath it I could see a ferocious mama-cat with her fangs dripping blood.

"She's a spoiled brat," I said. "She did it because she can't stand me." I knew I was making everything worse, but I couldn't help it.

"Now just wait," Daniel said, "and both of you be quiet. This is serving no purpose at all. Neither of you can handle yourselves tonight. I don't want to hear another word spoken in this house until breakfast tomorrow, when I hope we can speak to each other as if we're a family."

I knew that Daniel was trying to make it all right, but it was never going to work. That was for sure. The only thing I cared about was escaping upstairs to my room and getting away from the look in Joleen's mean little eyes.

Chapter Four

While Joleen and Daniel slept, I tiptoed down to the basement and got both my suitcases from the luggage bin. Then I packed everything but the things Joleen had bought me. It didn't seem right to take them. As soon as I saw Joleen's face last night I knew I had to leave. She looked at me as if I were a stranger who had come into her house to hurt her daughter; there was ice in her eyes.

As I packed I remembered something that Mimi had said to me before I left. "Try to fit in for a change, Sara Jo." Where had she expected me to fit? Into a family that was already made and complete? With a woman who thought me capable of murder? Not that I really blamed Joleen; the evidence was pretty well stacked against me.

I figured Mimi wasn't going to be exactly overjoyed to have me back either. What was I going to do for the rest of the summer? It would have been a lot easier to fool around with Katie than any of the kids I used to be friends with. At least Katie didn't worry about boys all day, every day.

And the pool! Wow, was I going to miss that pool.

When I finished packing, I was pretty calm because I knew I didn't have any choices. I had to go back to Boston, but I also knew that I wanted to apologize to Joleen before I left. Only I didn't know what I could say that would make anything different.

I fell asleep for a little while, and when I woke up I had a terrific idea. I'd make breakfast and surprise everyone. Maybe that would be a kind of an apology. Yeah, but what did I know about cooking breakfast?

Mimi usually made our meals. They consisted of vegetable, meat, and potato — plain, but I didn't mind. When Mimi's friend Thelma came for dinner, it was different. Mimi liked to show off for her, so we ate in the big dining room with candles, and had things like orange soufflés for dessert. Thelma's divorced. She has henna-rinsed hair that frizzles up all over her head, and she also has two kids who drive her crazy. One is heavy on punk rock and grass, and the other runs around with older men. Mimi once liked to show me off to Thelma as the ideally brought up young lady. How was she going to explain to her that I hadn't been a smash hit on Long Island?

There were some rolls in the breadbox, and I cut them open and spread the insides with strawberry jam and butter. I found fresh oranges, but I couldn't find the juicer, so I sliced them in half and squeezed until my knuckles turned white, and then I discovered ham steaks stacked up in the freezer, and I took three of them out.

Frizzled ham, I thought, suddenly remembering that

Joleen used to make it for us all the time. Even for dinner. But Harry hated that. Mimi never confused breakfast food with supper, and that suited him a lot better.

I heated the oven and wrapped everything in foil to keep it warm.

Hey, no mistakes. A pro, folks. Let's hear it for Sara Jo Jacoby, the Julia Child of Locust Valley. At least there was one thing I could do right at the Wertzburgers. And then Daniel came into the kitchen, wearing a blue terry robe that ended at his knees and let his hairy legs show. There was definitely a double standard about shaving in this country.

"What are you doing up, Sara Jo?" he asked as I started to set the table.

"I made breakfast for you."

"That was really thoughtful, honey." He sniffed. "It smells good."

I was nervous, waiting for Joleen to come down, and the dumb ninny dress I was wearing didn't make me feel any better. Little Miss Boston from twenty years ago. Mimi had picked it out. It had green and white checks and short puffy sleeves. Practically all my clothes look like that, but I'd never made much of a fuss about it because clothes had never been one of my great big interests. But right now, when I thought about the clothes I'd left behind upstairs, I started to feel really bad. Something had started to change inside me since I'd been here, only I wasn't going to be able to stay long enough to find out what it was.

As soon as Joleen came into the kitchen I jumped up and got very busy.

"Thanks, Sara, it was sweet of you to do this," she said as I carried the ham and the rolls dripping strawberry jam to the table. I couldn't tell anything from her voice.

Then as soon as I sat down, I knew something was missing. "The coffee! I forgot all about the coffee!"

"A tragedy," Joleen said. "You sit still and I'll make some instant."

As soon as she brought the coffee to the table, I screwed up my courage and started to talk. "About the finger paints and Lily," I began, and there was silence on either side of me. "I know I overreacted and I'm sorry. I really am. I didn't mean to hurt her." I sounded as if someone were accusing me. "I was downstairs with Katie, watching a horror movie, and I thought Lily was asleep. She was sleeping the last time I looked at her." I paused. "But the thing is, I got pretty involved in the movie, and when I looked for Lily again, she wasn't there." After that I started talking too fast and mixing my words up.

"Take it easy," Joleen said when I finally finished, "no one's blaming you."

I was glad to hear that. It meant that at least I could leave with a clear conscience. That is, if I could believe her. Maybe she'd say anything just to get rid of me fast.

"I was just wondering," I looked at them both, "when one of you could drive me to the airport? I've got all my things packed . . ." But I didn't want to leave now. I just wanted to pretend nothing had happened, and then I wanted to go to sleep for a while. Suddenly I was exhausted.

"Sara Jo, do you really want to go back to Boston?" Joleen put her hand on my arm, and I didn't jump away. I wanted her to touch me. I felt like crying. "You haven't even been here two weeks. I don't even know diddly-poop about you yet," she said.

"Well, I thought that I should, after everything that's happened." I paused and yawned. I thought I might even fall asleep at the table.

"Hey," Joleen ruffled my hair, "go upstairs and fall asleep, for ten hours at least."

And that's what I did. When I woke up, Joleen had kept dinner hot, and she told me that Lily was home and that she was fine. But I was glad she was asleep. I didn't want to face her yet.

That night I set my alarm for six-thirty so that I could call Mimi before she left for work. I wanted to catch her while she was doing the *Times* crossword puzzle and having her morning tea.

Mimi works for a big publishing company, writing promotion copy for novels and biographies. When I was younger, she used to bring uncorrected galleys home to see how many typographical errors I could catch, and I got really good at it.

When I was a kid I guess I got along pretty well with my aunt. As she put it, I used to "mind my p's and q's." I don't know what happened to change things around, but for a couple of years we've definitely been living in an armed-truce situation. She's old, and she's such a stick. There's a right way to do things and a wrong way, and, according to Mimi, I mostly pick the wrong way. But that morning I wanted to talk to her anyway. I was frightened about what I'd done, and I guess I was hoping she'd say that I was making a big deal over nothing, and that it was just an accident. But if I'd thought about it, I'd have known that Mimi wouldn't say anything like that. Maybe what I really hoped was that she'd understand and tell me not to worry. And that was really dumb of me, too.

Everyone was asleep, and I didn't want them to overhear me. I tiptoed downstairs and closed the den door quietly.

Mimi's voice sounded sleepy when the operator got on to ask if she would accept the charges.

Why should she still be in bed at seven o'clock? Because, a voice spoke into my ear, it's Saturday, you turkey.

Murder. Mimi hated anyone to wake her up. Absolutely *any*one, and that included her best friend, Thelma. She even wears these black shades over her eyes so the sun doesn't get to her before she's ready to face it.

"Sara Jo? Sara Jo, is that you?"

"It's me."

"Young lady, do you realize that it's seven o'clock on a Saturday morning?"

"I'm sorry, I forgot. I'll call you back later," I said.

"Well, I'm awake now. Why are you calling?"

Oh, wow. From the tone of my aunt's voice, I didn't want to tell her anything. When Mimi's in a bad mood, it's much better not to mess with her. Better to check back a couple of years later.

"What have you been doing down there in Locust Valley? I've been very concerned about you."

"What do you mean, what have I been doing?" I hedged. Was she psychic, or something?

"Well, I called to talk to you yesterday evening, but you were alseep, and then Joleen told me about the accident."

48

"You *know?*" I shrieked into the phone. "You already know about Lily?" It sounded like a conspiracy! "I wanted to tell you! I'm the one —"

"You are the one who'd better keep quiet, and right now, Sara Jo! By this time the Wertzburgers must think that I've been raising a little savage?"

Well, if that's how Mimi felt she could go and croak. As far as I was concerned, Mimi and I were *finito.*

"What happened to Lily was very unfortunate, and directly caused by your mismanagement."

I almost hated Mimi at that moment. She has never taken my part out of love. If she even loves me at all, I thought, it is still only out of some sense of duty to my father.

"I've already apologized," I told her. "But if you have any more suggestions, like shaving my head and entering a convent for the rest of the summer, just let me know." I hated everyone ganging up on me, whispering and plotting when I wasn't around.

"I don't care to pay for your sarcasm long distance, Sara."

"Fine." I stuck my tongue out into the phone like a five-year-old.

"One more thing." The old fart's voice was still zinging in my ear. "Joleen told me that you started your period."

"Yes. I did."

"Well, do you have all the things you'll need?"

What did she plan to do? Come rushing down here with another ancient copy of "Personally Yours"?

"You mean super Tampax? Sure. Joleen is keeping me supplied," I told her.

"All right, have your little joke, but please be sure you

49

behave yourself for the rest of the summer. I've had about all the bad reports I can handle."

I got hot with anger and embarrassment, but as soon as I realized that I was talking to a total stranger, I began to feel better. I was just furious at myself for calling her at all.

"I'm going to hang up now, Sara Jo, but I want you to sit down and write me a letter very soon. I want to know what's going on there with you."

When pigs grow on trees.

"Good-bye, Aunt Mimi. Sorry I woke you."

"Bye the bye for now, Sara." She always said that. What the hell did it mean?

When I got back to my room, I locked myself in. The only thing I wanted to do was hide. I got under the quilt, where it was almost dark, and cried.

Okay. Mimi didn't want to be associated with me anymore. Maybe she had never really wanted me at all. I was only this legacy from Harry. So what? She could put me in some girls' school in Maine, where I'd spend all my holidays and summer vacations. I'd wear itchy grey uniforms and study the lives of insects. I didn't care as long as she and I didn't have to rub up against each other anymore.

"Sara Jo?" I kicked off the quilt and tried to rub away my tears.

"Sara? You're in there, aren't you?"

I opened the door, and Joleen stood there, staring at me. Just what I needed. She'd want to know what was wrong, and I didn't feel like talking to anybody right now. My face must have been all splotched up from crying.

"What's the matter?" Her voice was soft, but I couldn't

tell her. She'd just think I was feeling sorry for myself. Boo hoo. Mimi doesn't like me anymore. As if that mattered.

"I just felt like crying," I said. "Nothing's wrong." Dumb-o answer. Why did I always have to sound so snotty?

"Do you want to talk? I have all day to talk," she said, sitting down on my wrecked bed.

I walked over to the dresser and fiddled with my hairbrush. I had known right away that Joleen had done this room over for me. But it was a room for a girl who had dates and went to parties. It wasn't a room to cry in, it was a room for dreaming. Soft mossy green walls, long white drapes, and a lounge chair with big floppy pillows.

"Ma—?" Lily was in the doorway, looking first at me, and then at Joleen.

I couldn't believe it when I saw her. She looked as if she'd been roughed around in a boxing ring. The whole left side of her head was streaked with crazy blue-and-red patterns, like she'd been attacked with finger paints.

I got down on my knees, but I knew Lily wouldn't come near me. And when I started to cry, she hid her head in Joleen's lap.

"Don't cry, Sara. It looks much worse than it really is."

And then when I didn't answer: "Why don't you wash your face and put on your bathing suit? Katie called a little while ago to tell you to come over for a swim." Joleen waited for me to say something.

"Okay, I will." Maybe I could hide underwater.

"But maybe first you'd like to tell me what's wrong? I think you were crying over more than Lily, weren't you?"

I nodded my head, feeling miserable.

"You know, sometimes it helps to share your feelings," she said, lifting Lily onto her lap. "I found that out late in life." She grinned at me. "See, I'm giving you the benefit of my experience. If you'd open up a little more it might help both of us, Sara."

"Help us what?" I stalled. She was getting to me when I was pretty low. I didn't know how much I could trust her, or how much I wanted to. Wasn't she always running off to call Mimi every time I burped? But when I looked at her I thought that maybe she did really care.

"Help us get closer."

"I had a fight on the phone with Mimi," I said, and then I heard Joleen sigh. "I can't stand Mimi." There. Now what would she say to that?

"She means to do the right thing," Joleen said, trying. "It's difficult for her."

"I knew you'd back her up, and you don't even know what the fight was about, right? So let's just skip it." I was getting angry. Sometimes Joleen and I would start to get a little closer, and then something would just snap and we'd lose it.

"I wasn't 'backing up' anybody, Sara Jo. I just know how difficult things can be sometimes —"

"You mean how difficult I can be. That's what you really mean, so why don't you say it?" I had to be careful because I was afraid I was going to start crying again.

"I didn't say it because it wasn't what I meant."

"I don't want to talk about anything now," I said, and my voice cracked a little.

Joleen got up and put her arms around me, and I stiffened my shoulders. I didn't want her holding me, I felt too awful to be touched. Finally, she dropped her arms. "We'll talk about this when you feel more like it," she said. "Believe it or not, I'm on your side."

After she left, I took a shower, and while I was drying myself, I heard her call me from downstairs.

"What?" I wrapped a pale pink towel around me. A towel definitely meant for the young prom queen living in my room. It felt like velvet, and had a satin band down the center. There was a call for me. Was it Mimi, wanting me to forgive her? Ha.

I picked up the extension in Joleen and Daniel's room.

"Hello?"

"Hello, Sara."

"Daniel? How come you're calling me?"

"Because I want to ask you a question, kiddo. That's why."

"What question?"

"I'd like to know if you'll have dinner with me tonight."

"Why?" Alarm bells went off in my ears. Something was wrong.

"Is that enthusiasm I hear in your voice, Sara Jo?"

"Something's the matter," I finally said.

"Well, just a little wrong," he agreed slowly. "I think we need to talk some things out."

Oh, God.

"All right," I said, sighing. Did I have a choice?

"Hey, Sara, you might enjoy it," he said, teasing.

"Sure."

They've decided they're going to ease me out after all, I thought. It had just taken them a while to make up their minds, and Joleen hadn't had the guts to tell me herself. Besides, Daniel was the original Mr. Nice, so he'd do a better job of smoothing everything out and explaining how this summer just wasn't going to work. When Joleen couldn't handle something, she ran away from it, and now she had Daniel to do her dirty work for her. That thought made me feel low, really black.

On the way back to my room, I passed Lily's door. I could hear her in there making lip-smacking noises while she was supposed to be taking a nap. Actually, she was sitting up in her playpen with an alphabet book on her lap.

I walked into the room. "Lily?"

She stood up and threw her book at me.

"I'd do the same thing if I were you," I told her, picking up the book and giving it back to her. "Do you want me to read to you, Lily?"

"No."

"Yeah, I figured you'd say that."

I reached out to gently touch her head, and she stayed very still. I traced a line of vermillion past her temple and into her snaky curls.

"Lily hurt."

I pulled my hand away quickly.

"No, no, Sara. She didn't mean that you hurt her." Joleen had sneaked up behind me.

"Lily, why don't you let Sara Jo read you a story?"

That's what I mean when I say Joleen's pushy. You smile at her and she sits on your head and tells you what to do for the rest of the afternoon. Now she wanted me to make nice to Lily.

54

It wasn't until I got back to my room that I realized I was still wearing Junior Deb's towel. In Boston we got wrapped up like mummies before we put even a foot into the hallway. What was going on with me?

Chapter Five

I decided that I wouldn't think about anything but the indigo pool and swimming around inside it for the rest of the day, because whenever my thoughts drifted to Daniel and what he was probably going to tell me at dinner, I got the shivers and started to feel sick to my stomach.

Katie's back gate was open, and without looking around I sailed right through and jumped into the water, shouting, "Here comes the mermaid extraordinaire!" as I went. The water felt cool and wonderful against my skin, but as I fought my way up to the surface I heard someone laughing, like the sound of little bells tinkling in the wind. I knew right away that it wasn't Katie or Clovis. No indeed.

Then when I got the water out of my eyes and looked up I saw this blond beauty lying out on the diving board. Everything about her was perfect, from her honey-colored hair to her long tan legs and the coral bathing suit she wore that showed off every bit of her curvy body to absolute perfection. Just looking at her made me uncomfortable, aware of my bony arms, skinny chest, and the fact that I hardly ever wear lipstick. What, I wondered, was this cheerleader and homecoming queen doing sunning herself on the Delaneys' diving board? Whatever it was, I wished she'd disappear. Girls who could look like that definitely gave me an inferiority complex.

Katie was hanging onto the side of the pool, churning up froth by practicing kicks with her feet. She was attacking the water viciously and she wouldn't even look at me, so I did a sidestroke over to her and grabbed on to the side of the pool.

"Hi, remember me?" I said, with my back to the beauty queen. "There's an alien on your diving board," I whispered.

"Yeah," she said, still kicking, "I know."

"Katie?" I splashed water into her face. "Who is it?"

"Who is who?" She gave me a mean look and then, as if she'd just understood, said, "Oh, yeah, her. Sara Jo," she said reluctantly, "this is my cousin. Taffy."

Taffy?

"Hi," the beauty queen called out as I made myself turn to look at her again. "You must be Katie's little friend."

And how old was she supposed to be? I wondered, hoisting myself out of the pool and getting the water out of my suit. I thought maybe I'd go back to Joleen's, not that I was looking forward to that, but it might be better than struggling to make conversation with Taffy. I did not get along well with the Taffys of this world.

"What's the matter with you?" Katie asked me. "Aren't you even going to swim?" She sounded mad.

"Well, I am." Taffy got up, stretched, and then ran her hands down the sides of her body as if she were caressing her-

57

self. "You can put some lotion on my back when I get out, okay, Kat-Kins?"

"I can hardly wait," Katie said nastily as Taffy jumped twice on the board and then cut into the water with a perfect swan dive.

I sat down on the side of the pool and stared at my wavy underwater legs. I didn't really want to go home. Maybe I could stick it out with Katie, who didn't look like she was having much fun, either.

"You're going to wear your legs out, Kat-Kins," I said, sliding in next to her. "So who is this Taffy person?"

She let go of the side of the pool and we both started to tread water while Taffy did perfect laps on the other side of the pool.

"I told you," Katie said, "she's my cousin, and when I grow up I'm supposed to be just like her." She batted her eyes at me through her fishbowl glasses and I started to giggle.

"Why don't you like her?" I asked.

"Because she's dumb." Katie lifted one hand and smacked at the water. "The only thing she can think about and talk about are all the guys who are in love with her and her perfectly perfect body, and my mother just happens to have picked *her* out to be my role model. That's why I'm mad, okay? And to follow in good ole Taffy's example, this fall my mother is enrolling me in the same dumb charm school Taffy went to when she was my age!"

"How old is she anyway?" Katie really did have problems.

"Seventeen, and boys have been after her since she was

about three. Yuck," Katie said, and just then Taffy popped out of the water between the two of us.

"Hey, cousin," she said, grabbing Katie around the waist and trying to pull her under. "Do your dead body for me."

"I'm not in the mood." Katie kicked away and held onto the side of the pool again.

Taffy was even prettier close up, and I wondered if she put Vaseline on her teeth to get them to sparkle like that.

I didn't know what to say, and whenever I don't know what to say I usually get a little weird and silly.

"Go on, Kat-Kins," I said, "do your dead body. Maybe it'll be better than your live body. Let me see."

"It's just a stupid dead man's float, that's all it is," Katie said. "And will you quit calling me Kat-Kins?"

"Okay, Katy-Did, whatever you say," I said, which won me a look from Katie that said I was vermin. Then she swam to the steps of the pool and climbed out.

"I'm going inside," she told us angrily, slapping her wet feet down on the cement as if she meant to punish something.

Oh no, I thought, don't leave me alone out here with *her*. But Katie was gone, and I knew I deserved it.

"That just leaves you, Sara Jo." Taffy gave me one of her dazzling smiles. Girls like her flirted with everyone.

"Leaves me for what?"

"Will you do my back, hon? I'm wearing this super dress tonight, and my back isn't the same color as my front." Boy, did she have problems. She screwed up her forehead and I wondered if she were going to cry about it.

"You'd better get out of the water," I told her. "Your fingers are getting wrinkled."

She held up one hand and stared. "Oh, murder. Come on, Sara Jo, I really need you to help me. Please?" She sounded soft as a kitten, and she was pouting a little. Boys probably flipped over that.

What was I supposed to do? Because I wasn't sure, I followed her out of the pool and when she handed me the bottle of suntan lotion I smeared some of it on her back, but I felt like a real dope doing it.

"Make sure you get it on evenly," she said. "I want the color to be perfect."

For the next fifteen minutes I listened to Taffy, who carried on a nonstop monologue, and I realized that Katie was definitely right. Her cousin was one bubblehead. All she could talk about were boys, clothes, makeup, and boys. She was just a slightly older version of the kids I used to hang out with at home, only she was more empty-headed than they were. When I looked into Taffy's eyes it was like nothing at all was going on behind them, as if I could see the sky right through her head. The thing was, though, that she was so obsessed with herself that she kind of fascinated me. She probably knew everything there was to know about boys and dates, and I suddenly wished I had the courage to ask her some questions, although I knew I never would. Some things you just have to figure out for yourself.

"You know what would be nice?" she said, turning her head on the chaise longue to look at me for the first time.

"What?"

"It would be nice if Aunt Clovis would let us take a sun bath in the nude, you know? Then I could be the same shade all over. Wouldn't that be terrific?"

Terrific for you, maybe, I thought, but I'd rather step off the top of the Empire State Building.

"You're in trouble," I told her. "You're getting red as a lobster."

"I am?" Taffy looked at her back and then she jumped up and put her robe on.

"You'll probably be peeling all over the place by tonight," I said because I couldn't resist.

"Oh, no. Damn," she moaned, belting the robe tightly and looking at me as if I was responsible. "You should have warned me sooner. I have a date tonight with Hank." She said it as if I knew who she was talking about.

"Who's Hank?"

"My boyfriend. He's great." Her face got dreamy. "Oh, don't you just love men, Sara Jo?"

"Yeah," I said, "I adore them." I was beginning to get bored, and I realized that a little of Taffy could stretch a long way. Hey, that wasn't bad. I'd have to remember it to tell Katie.

"Who do you go out with?" she asked me.

"Me? I go out with myself mostly. Or if I don't, I stay home. I often stay home with myself, too."

"What?" she blinked at me.

"I don't date," I explained. "I have bad breath."

"You *do*?"

"I was only kidding, Taffy," I said, getting up. I wanted

to go in and find Katie. I hoped that she wasn't mad at me, because Katie was a lot more fun and a lot more interesting to be with than her cousin.

"I bet it's your hair," Taffy said suddenly, stopping me.

"What's my hair?" I grabbed a bunch of red frizz and pulled at it, feeling awkward.

"You ought to have a body wave or something," Taffy said. "It just grows out all wild from your head."

"Thanks, I'll remember that. But right now, I kind of like the rusty Brillo look, you know?"

Taffy shook her head. "Guys might like you if you paid a little more attention to the way you look." Now she was looking me up and down, very carefully, and I was embarrassed.

"Excuse me," I told her, "but I have to find Katie." And then I escaped into the house.

I found out then that it wasn't easy to apologize to Katie. When she was mad, she was like cement.

"Katie, you're making it very difficult for me to tell you I'm sorry."

"So what?" she asked me in a tough little voice.

"I'm trying to tell you that I didn't mean to call you those things, and that I really am sorry."

"Sorry-schmorry," she said in a singsong voice, and I didn't have a lot of hope for our conversation.

I sat down on one of her hooked rugs. She had lots of them, all made by Clovis. This one was a brown cocker spaniel against a red background. I figured I might as well sit because it looked like I was going to be there for a while.

"So you must really like Taffy, huh?" Katie was looking over my head at a huge panda poster from the Washington Zoo. "You spent the whole afternoon talking to her, and by the way, Sara Jo, you're not supposed to sit on these rugs with wet clothes on."

I snapped my fingers. "I knew it! Another Delaney!"

"No, it's not. It's just something about the kind of wool my mother uses. It could shrink or something," Katie said. Pause. "What about Taffy?"

"What about her?" I asked. "She's a space cadet. But she's pretty. She certainly is pretty."

"Sara, nobody knows how pretty she is better than ole Taf," Katie informed me. "You planning to be her best friend now, or something?"

Then I got mad.

"You know, Katie, you're acting just like a little kid, you really are. You left me out there with that nerd, and I had to listen to her and then put suntan lotion all over her. You think I was having fun?"

"Well, you certainly stayed out there with her for long enough. No one asked you to stay out there for so long. What was she doing? Teaching you all her beauty secrets?"

"I'm going home," I told her. "I've had it."

"So what's at home?" Katie said, trying to stall me.

"I have to get dressed. I'm having dinner with Daniel," I told her, in a voice that I was trying to make sound deb.

"Just you and Mr. Wertzburger?" She sounded impressed.

"Yeah," I grinned. "He has a thing for my bod."

"Sara Jo, that isn't even funny!"

"Can I help it if older men are attracted to me?"

63

I walked home slowly because I wanted time to think about Katie and me. I wondered if she and I were really going to be good friends. Even though she was younger, I liked her a lot, and it had been a long time since I'd had a really close girl friend.

But I knew I'd have to be careful. My problem is that when I really like someone, I sort of dive in with my eyes closed. I want to spend all my time with them and stuff like that. That's how it was when I had this thing for my science teacher, Mr. Sacks. He's bald, and he has a roly-poly stomach, and he always used to tell me that I was super-terrific at chemistry. Sometimes he'd even stay after school and help me with projects. Once he said that I ought to be the one helping him out because I probably knew more about splitting the atom than he did. That really made me feel great, and after that I spent as much time as I could around him.

I really loved Mr. Sacks, but I made a pretty stupid mistake with him. One day I asked him, half kidding, but I really meant it, if he wanted to adopt me. Sara Jo Sacks. I must have been crazy! Well, it turned out that Mr. Sacks got pretty upset. Maybe he was afraid that I was going to accuse him of molesting me or something. I had to see this counselor, and the school called Mimi up for a conference. The upshot was that my aunt decided I'd be better off in a different school next year. I was finished at Needlewood.

When I got home, I found a bag from Saks on my bed, and it was filled with new bras and bikini panties. The finger paints hadn't all come out of the other ones. I wanted to go downstairs and thank Joleen. It really had been a nice thing for her to do, but I didn't want to see her right now. If they were planning to get rid of me, and this was a good-bye present. . . . No, I wouldn't say anything. Not yet.

I went downstairs at seven o'clock, and Daniel had just finished giving instructions to the sitter, who was about fifteen, with a streaky blond ponytail and purple lipstick.

"Are you ever going to look like that, Sara Jo?" he asked me as we got into the car.

People can really ask you some ridiculous questions. But then I decided that Daniel was probably as nervous as I was. Not that I felt sorry for him or anything. After all, he just had this one unpleasant job to do and then he could wash his hands of the whole situation. I was the one who was about to be tossed out.

"How come you got a sitter, anyway?" I said. "Where's Joleen tonight?"

"She went to an AA meeting."

"Oh."

"Do you know about Alcoholics Anonymous, Sara Jo?"

"Sure. Doesn't everybody?"

He laughed. "I doubt it. Your mother is a very special woman, you know. She's been through a lot." Then he reached over, took my hand, and squeezed it. "But so have you, Sara."

Yeah, I thought, and I have a lot more to go through tonight, too.

We ate at a restaurant with a gristmill churning in a pond outside our window.

Daniel ordered a martini, and that made me remember that

65

Harry once said Joleen bought her courage out of a bottle. Maybe that's what Daniel was doing, having a drink so he'd be brave enough to dump his stepdaughter.

It was obvious to me when he finally decided that he was ready to say what was on his mind. He got a stern look on his face, and he just kept looking at me without saying a word. I began to get frightened. I wished he'd just say it and get it over with. It was the waiting that was the killer.

I remembered feeling like that before, with my father. I guess I was about seven, and I thought it was a great idea to put food coloring in a great big tank of tropical fish he had. By mixing the colors I could make the water turn a bright, beautiful purple. Like an ocean in a fairy tale. But Harry was furious because he had to drain and refill his humongous tank. He accused me of doing it maliciously, but I didn't even know what the word meant.

He called me into his den and said he was going to punish me. And then he told me I should go upstairs to my room and wait for him.

Harry let me wait for two hours. Then he came upstairs and told me what my punishment was. I don't even remember what he said, but I remember those two hours I sat on my bed waiting for him to come up to my room.

Daniel took a sip from his drink. "Sara Jo." It was coming. "I think Joleen and I might have you at a disadvantage."

I didn't know what he was talking about.

"During the last few years we've learned an awful lot about you."

What was this, a spy ring? Oh, yeah. Mimi the mouth.

My foot kept falling asleep, which always happened when I got nervous.

"Joleen had missed so many years of you that when she got well, she wanted to know all the bits and pieces of Sara Jo growing up, and you wouldn't let her do that. You never answered her letters, and after a while your father didn't want to have very much to do with her, either. He kept saying it was your decision, and that you didn't want to see her. So she had only one other alternative. Your Aunt Mimi. At first, Mimi wouldn't even talk to her on the phone, and she didn't answer any of your mother's letters, either." He laughed. "But Joleen was very persistent, and eventually she learned all about you from Mimi. Actually, Mimi's been keeping us filled in on you for a long time now, and it seemed only fair that we should tell you about that, Sara. I wanted to do it." He smiled. "Sometimes you and your mother strike a lot of sparks between you. That's natural for now, but I thought maybe I could make this understandable to you."

By now my foot had reached that numb point where it really hurts, and then my fingers started to tingle, too.

Daniel had been talking and talking about how Mimi had finally told Joleen this or that, but who cared? Obviously my whole life was an open book now, but I wasn't even listening, until we got to the Key lime pie for dessert, and I heard Daniel say, "Mr. Sacks," and then I dropped my fork.

"None of that is any of your business, Daniel," I said, and my voice was shaking.

"Honey, I'm explaining all this to you because Joleen and I want everything to be very honest and open with you. I hope what I said will help you understand how much you matter to Joleen, and to me too."

Sure. I mattered so much to Joleen that it took her almost my whole life to realize it. What was I supposed to do? Joleen just didn't *feel* like my mother.

"Is there anything you'd like to ask me or talk to me about, Sara Jo?"

"Like what?"

"Like how you're feeling now."

"I'm feeling silent," I said. And that was all I said.

On the way home I thought about Mimi. About how she'd been in cahoots with Joleen for years without my knowing, giving her a report card on my behavior. Boy, I bet Mimi had been hoping that I'd wow them down in Locust Valley so she could get rid of me. But by now Joleen must have thoroughly disenchanted her, and Mimi would be in a frazzle because she hadn't been able to unload me.

The house looked cozy as we drove up the driveway. It looked the way a house is supposed to look. Nestled in pine trees, with lights glowing behind the curtains. Unfortunately, we were not exactly your basic hot dog and apple pie American family, but I guessed I wouldn't mind spending the rest of the summer there. Especially with Katie's pool right next door. It would be better than the alternative — my aunt Mimi.

"Sara? Why don't you stay and talk for a while?" Joleen had just gotten home.

I wasn't tired, but I didn't want to be part of one of Joleen's punch and cookies parties, either. So I made myself a tuna fish sandwich and started up the back stairs.

"Can't," I said, hurrying up the stairs before she could stop me.

After I got undressed, I put on my bathing suit and lay down to wait until it was late enough for me to sneak into the Delaneys' pool. I wanted to be all alone in the water at night.

By twelve-fifteen I was walking silently across the lawn with the sunflower cap in my hand. At least that was one Delaney I didn't have to break.

It was dark and peaceful as I slid into the water, and then a cloud drifted away and a pale path of moon lighted the pool. From the other side of the water Joleen grinned at me like a fellow conspirator. I almost died!

"I just had a feeling you'd be here," she whispered when we met in the middle of the pool.

What was she trying to do, follow me wherever I went? But then I realized she couldn't have followed me — she'd been there ahead of me. It was weird.

"I love the water at night," she said, "but I'm a little guilty about breaking what must be at least twenty Delaneys."

"At least," I said. "Well, so long." I turned onto my stomach to do a crawl over to the side of the pool.

"Sara Jo, stay here for a while with me, will you?"

"I can't," I said. "It's too cold and I'm getting a cramp in my leg."

"Why do you always try to escape when I want to talk to you?" she asked me in a loud whisper.

"Why can't you give me any privacy?" I said, feeling close to tears. For someone who hardly ever cried, I'd been doing a lot of it for these past few weeks.

"I'm sorry." Joleen swam close to me. "I wanted to explain a little more. About Mimi and —"

"Not tonight," I said, hissing, and then I started to cry. "Please!" I got out of the pool and ran.

When I finally got into bed that night I was still crying and I was also shivering all over. What I wanted most in the world was for someone to hold me, only I couldn't figure out who I wanted that someone to be.

Chapter Six

A few days later, Joleen finally got me.

"Sara Jo, I'd like to borrow some of your time today. There's something I want to talk to you about."

She sure had lousy timing. I was on my way over to Katie's to see if she wanted to go to the movies. It was a blistering, hot day, and the humidity alone had already broken a record. I was thinking of icy cold air, cherry soda, and popcorn.

"What is it?" I sat down at the kitchen table and pushed some crumbs around.

"Would you like some apple juice? I just made a fresh pitcher."

"No thanks." I felt trapped.

She poured juice for herself and then sat down near me. "Daniel said he blew the whole Mimi thing with you. He really felt bad about it, Sara. He said you didn't say very much, but your eyes looked frozen, and I knew just what he meant. I used to be able to freeze my eyes up, too. Mostly when I wanted to block off my ears."

"I wasn't blocking off anything," I told her, "and I don't care if you and Mimi got to be palsy-walsy. So you wanted to find out all about me. Terrific. Mimi has a big mouth, and that's her problem. Now I guess the two of you get to talk on the phone every day, trading Sara Jo stories. It sounds boring to me, but if that's what you want to do, fine. Now, if you'll excuse me —"

"Okay," Joleen said. "I give up. Now you tell me what to do so you'll approve of me, Sara Jo. Frankly, every way I turn with you seems to be the wrong way."

Joleen Wertzburger's luck had just run out.

"Look, I will tell you what to do," I said. "Would you just leave me alone, and give me some space? You're always on top of me!" I stood up and stared down at her with my frozen eyes, and then I turned and walked out of the kitchen. What an exit. It should have made me feel terrific, only it didn't.

The next evening I had a visit from Joleen. At dinner, with Daniel at the hospital, we'd been cool and polite. Lily was a distraction, pounding the table legs with a wooden spoon and tying knots in my sneaker laces. Lily and I had gotten to be a little friendlier with each other lately.

At about eight o'clock, Joleen knocked on my open door.

I looked up. "You can come in."

"I won't interrupt for too long, Sara Jo, but you've been complaining about your hair, and I wondered if you'd like to do anything about it."

"Do what?"

"Go to the beauty parlor and have them do whatever you want."

The problem was I didn't know what I wanted. The problem was that Joleen had more style than anyone I knew, and she probably would be able to give me some terrific advice, but I was too stubborn to ask her for it.

And now she was waiting for me to say something.

"Thanks a lot," I told her. That was the most I could manage.

"Okay. Do you want me to make an appointment for you tomorrow?"

"I can't tomorrow. I'm doing something with Katie."

"Sara, I wish you'd check your plans out with me first. Just a request."

"Well, I will from now on," I said politely.

"Shall I make the appointment for Thursday?"

"Yeah, okay."

"I have a suggestion." Joleen stopped on her way to the door, setting off danger alarms.

"What is it?"

"Don't let them shave off all those beautiful curls. Tell them to show you how to handle them — a different style, maybe." She smiled. "You do have incredible hair."

"That's one way of putting it," I said.

"You'll change your mind." Joleen smiled.

Katie and I were supposed to go to the movies together the next afternoon, but we never got there because we stopped to have a soda first, and then we ended up talking right through the afternoon matinee.

It started off with Katie telling me how lucky I was to have Joleen for a mother.

"She's really excellent, you know that, Sara Jo?" Katie had a chocolate mustache around her mouth and she really looked cute, but I wasn't exactly amused by what she was saying.

"It's not a word I would have thought of," I said, spooning up butterscotch sauce.

"That's because you have this dumb chip on your shoulder. Every time Mrs. Wertzburger is around, you get all weird and start acting like —"

"Like *what*?" I asked angrily. "What do I act like?"

"And now you're getting mad at me. What did I do? That's how you get — just like that, with your mother. Like these great big thorns start growing out of you, and you have this giant sign around your neck that reads, 'Don't touch! Don't get any closer or I'll fang you apart with my sharp ole teeth!' Like that." She finished drinking her shake as if she hadn't just dumped a load of bricks right down on my head.

"Thank you, Dr. Delaney, shrink junior-grade," I said sarcastically. "Whenever I need couch treatment I'll be sure to look you up."

"Don't get mad, Sara Jo. Please?"

I pushed the glasses back up on her nose. "What's the matter with your own mother?"

"Clovis? Nothing." She shrugged. "Except that she's all over me every minute for just about everything. But your mother isn't like that. We used to talk sometimes, and she really understood everything I told her. She would just sit and listen in this very careful way, and then she'd tell me what she thought. Not as if I were some kind of dumb kid or anything, but like we were kind of — you know, equals. . . . I guess that sounds kind of funny."

"The whole thing sounds kind of 'funny.' Your friend, Mrs. Wertzburger, is on top of me *all* the time."

But Katie was shaking her head. "It isn't her. It's you, Sara Jo. Every time she opens her mouth you practically take her head off."

I didn't know what to say, but there was something bothering me, making me uncomfortable.

"So are you mad at me now?" Katie said.

"I'm still considering."

"You're not, because you know I'm right." Katie was smug.

I ignored her and took a big swallow of soda. End of conversation.

Chapter Seven

Joleen had made my appointment for one o'clock, and I was nervous as soon as I woke up.

"Is anyone going with you to Maurice's?" she asked as I came into the kitchen. She was harnessing Lily into her jump seat.

"Sarry jump Lily now!"

I went over and bounced her into the air. "Is that high enough for you?" I asked her. She really was a pretty cute kid.

"Sara Jo, how come you never answer a question the first time it's asked?" Joleen said.

"I didn't hear you. What did you say?"

"I asked if someone was going to Maurice's with you."

I hadn't known what to do. I'd thought about asking Katie, but I figured she'd get bored and start doing crazy things like sitting under a dryer and pretending she was frying up alive. I really wanted Joleen to come with me, but it would never work. She'd get bossy, and then we'd fight. No way, José, I decided.

"I'd rather go alone," I told her. But it wasn't the truth.

Maurice's salon was decorated in red velvet, with gold braid and crystal chandeliers; and even the people who did things like sweeping up hair and arranging curlers wore uniforms and spoke with an accent.

I was intimidated as soon as I walked up to the reception desk and an elegant woman came out and pulled a gold dressing gown around my shoulders. Sara Jo, queen for a day, I thought, feeling my soul quiver. Then she stood back to admire me.

"*Voilà!* Now we begin."

And so we did. First with a facial, which was a whole new experience for me. I saw all the great big holes in my face get cleaned out, and the girl who bruised my skin raw told me my pores wouldn't clog up again if I'd rub apricot grits into my face every night. Every night? I saw that trying to get beautiful and stay that way could be a very serious, time-consuming business. Taffy probably devoted her life to going over every inch of herself on a daily basis. Katie told me that one pimple would reduce Taffy to tears! I could never care about my body like that, could I? I wondered as I lay under a lamp with a heavy mass of black gop drying on my face. No, I decided, feeling my skin shrink under the mask, but maybe I'd start paying a little more attention. I mean, it wasn't until today at Maurice's that I'd realized my eyebrows grew in a straight line across my nose.

I thought about the kids back home, squealing if they noticed an errant hair that needed to be plucked or a chip in their nail polish. That kind of slavish devotion to the picture they'd make had turned me off them as much as their going

77

ape shit any time a pimply-faced boy walked by. But now while all these things were being done to repair me, I thought maybe it wasn't all that awful. Maybe when Maurice's got finished with me, I'd at least have a basis to begin with. A New Look, I fantasized.

I was almost dozing under the lamp when the face of Taffy the homecoming queen swam before me, and for the first time I conceded that it might be fun to at least try to look a little better. Occasionally anyhow.

My hair was the big production. A whole group gathered around to discuss me.

"*Chérie!* We rinse this red, no?"

"I think it was red when I came in," I said, but I sounded feeble. These people were the experts, and I'd given myself over entirely to their care.

"But no, it is now dull. We will give life."

It was then that I decided I wasn't going to look in a mirror until I got home. I would not stare at myself while everyone else was staring at me. This was personal, and I was going to look and rejoice in private.

Just before I got under the dryer, Pierre, the hair stylist, pinched my elbow to tell me there was a telephone call for me. He personally led me to the phone, which was in a little alcove covered by a gold mesh curtain.

"Hello?"

"Hello, Sara. How's it going?" Joleen asked.

"I don't know. It's okay, I guess."

"What's wrong?"

"Nothing."

"Does your hair look nice?"

"I don't know how it looks." I sighed, losing energy. What if I came out with a head I didn't recognize? What if I looked like a freak?

"What do you mean, you don't know how it looks?"

"It has goo and gop and crap all over it. It's wound around steel and covered up with plastic, so how could I know how it looks?" I was talking too loud, but I wasn't really angry with Joleen, I was just very nervous.

"All right, Sara. I won't argue with you. I just called to tell you that I got an emergency call from AA, and I have to go out. I'm leaving Lily with Clovis, and you'll have to take a bus home. Do you have money with you?"

"Yes. Do you want me to pick Lily up?"

"No, I'll stop for her on my way home."

So she didn't trust me. That hurt. And then I wondered what an AA emergency could be. Maybe somebody had swallowed the cork from a wine bottle. Well, it was none of my business.

When I pushed the mesh curtain aside, an attendant came dancing up, and I let her lead me to my own private dryer where I baked for almost an hour. When my hair was finally being combed out, I stared at my lap, refusing to look in the mirror.

Before I left everyone made a big fuss over me.

"*Magnifique!*" Pierre kept saying. "Magnificent!"

It couldn't be all bad, then, I told myself.

Finally, they presented me with a large see-through plastic bag, filled with shampoo, conditioners, picks, and little tortoiseshell combs.

Just before I went out the door, Pierre kissed me on both

cheeks, and whispered, "Lovely, lovely," in my ear.

As soon as I got to the Wertzburgers, Katie and Taffy pedaled up the drive and hopped off their bikes.

Exactly the two people I didn't want to see yet. I wanted to get used to my new look alone.

"Look at your hair!" Katie yelled.

And that's what they both did until I thought I was going to scream.

"It isn't that bad, is it?"

Taffy giggled. "Well, it sure is different," she said, making me want to smack the dumb grin off her face.

"I have to get used to it, but I think it's neato," Katie told me, only she wasn't looking at me. She was looking down at her feet.

"Excuse me," I said. "I'm going in."

"Hey, wait," Katie called out.

"What is it?" I didn't turn around.

"We came over to tell you Lily's supposed to have dinner with us if Mrs. Wertzburger doesn't get home." Katie paused. "And you too."

"No, thank you," I said, and walked inside.

Where was the handiest mirror? And then I remembered — on the door of the hall closet. I turned on the light.

God. I didn't want to believe what I was seeing. It was terrible! I looked like a freak.

My hair was almost crimson! Even though it was only a rinse, I still looked like a newly painted fire engine. I just couldn't believe it. Why did they want to make a punk rock star out of me?

Worst of all was the way my hair was cut. There were all

these little curlicues scattered around my head, making it look like a collection of Junior Slinkies. I could even make them pop in and out just by moving forward and back. Lily would love it. I could chop off my head and let her play with it all day.

I went into the living room to get the beauty bag that I hoped would wash all the crap out when the doorbell rang. No way was I going to let anyone in.

"Sara Jo? Sara Jo, I have to talk to you. Please!" Katie called. "Come on, let me in. I thought we were friends!"

I went over and unlocked the door.

"Hi." She looked like a little scrubbed kid in her shorts and polo shirt. "I'm sorry, Sara Jo, honest." Katie was nibbling on her lip, and then she looked straight at me. "How come you did it?"

"I didn't think I'd look like this," I told her miserably. "I was vying for the title of Miss Junior Deb America." It cost me a lot to try and joke with her because I was pretty close to tears.

"Can't you wash it out? Or did they dye it?" she asked, picking around between the Slinkies.

"No, it's only a rinse," I said gloomily.

"Sara Jo, that's great! Just go upstairs and wash it until the color goes away."

"It's not that easy, Katie. It's supposed to last for months."

"Why don't you just go up and try it, huh?" Katie said.

"All right, all right. Don't be so bossy," I told her. But I was really glad she was there.

I stood under the needle shower spray until my skin started to break out in giant white puckers. By the time the water in the tub was sloshing against my knees I'd used up an entire bottle of shampoo.

"You're going to drown!" Katie called in to me.

She was right. I wrapped a towel around me and stepped out into the steaming bathroom. How had I ever thought I was going to be transformed into some kind of beauty? I wanted to die.

"How does it look?" I asked Katie.

"I can't tell," she said. "It's too wet." So I took another towel and spent a long time rubbing my hair to get it as dry as I could.

"Oh, it's lots better," Katie said.

But she lied.

"It's awful."

"Come on, let's go downstairs, Sara Jo. Don't worry about it. It'll wash out eventually."

Sure, but by that time I'd be too old to care.

I brushed my hair straight back, but in seconds all the little corkscrews popped up again, and the color was still terrible. Those millions of shampoos hadn't done anything at all.

"You want some lemonade, Katie?" I said, trying to rev up our spirits. "I think Joleen just made some."

"I can't," Katie said, "I have to have dinner. Clovis doesn't like it if I eat anything first."

"Katie, this is lemonade. You don't have to chew it."

Then I had an idea. I felt like doing something wild, and I knew just what it was.

"Forget the lemonade," I told her. "Let's go straight for the strong stuff."

"Huh?" Katie pushed the glasses up on her nose and looked puzzled.

"I'll show you in a minute," I said, heading for the dining room.

I came back with a bottle of gin and a bottle of vermouth.

"Sara Jo, what are you going to do with those? You're crazy! That's liquor. I don't want to drink liquor, it tastes terrible." Katie made a gagging sound and stuck her tongue out of her mouth as far as it would go.

"I'm going to whip up some martinis," I said, getting a pitcher down from the cupboard. It was the one drink I knew how to make because my father and Mimi used to have them on holidays, or sometimes when they had company. I'd watched Harry make them plenty of times, and as I poured the gin into the pitcher I suddenly remembered something he'd said about Joleen when she'd been drinking: "She's feeling no pain tonight."

Absolutely terrific, I thought, adding vermouth to the gin and stirring both together, because I am right now in the place where I don't want to feel any more pain.

I took two glasses from the shelf and poured, trying to ignore Katie shrieking at me in the background.

"Have a little before-dinner cocktail, dear," I said, handing her a glass. "It will improve your appetite."

Katie shook her head. "No way," she said.

"Why not?" I asked. "Is that another Delaney?" I took a sip. Not so bad. Not so good, but not so terrible either. Maybe it's like olives, I thought. You just have to get used to the taste.

"If it's not a Delaney now, it will be," Katie said. "I don't think my mother has even thought about me drinking yet."

"So you're not breaking a rule. Just try it, Katie, come on." I edged the glass closer to her. "It's nice. Very smooth."

Finally she picked up the glass and took a tiny sip.

"Good, right?" But Katie had started to clutch her throat and gag.

"What's the matter?" I whammed her on the back. Her glasses were hanging from one ear, and her eyes were watering.

"Sara, don't do that!" she choked.

"It's excellent," I said. That was a lie but I was determined to keep trying until the pain went away. I wondered how long that would take.

"You're crazy, Sara Jo. Stop drinking that stuff!" Katie was really upset.

"They're good. Come on, Katie, try again."

"You'd better not have any more or you'll be sorry, Sara Jo," she warned me.

"Why will I be sorry?" I asked, taking another swallow.

"You'll get drunk!"

I was already starting to feel mellow. Not bad. I was even beginning to forget about the horror sitting on top of my head. Even better.

"How do you know if you're drunk?" I asked Katie. But how would she know? I would just have to wait and ask Mama Joleen. Just then the phone rang.

"The Wertzburgers are not available for discussion at the moment. At the sound of the —"

"Is that you on the line, Sara Jo, dear?"

Clovis. She always made me feel as if I were a basket case.
"It's me, Mrs. Delaney."

"Just making sure. All right, now, will you send Katie home for dinner, please? And you're more than welcome to come along with her, Sara."

"Oh, no, but thank you kindly." I almost cracked up.

"Sup-sup-suppertime, Katie," I said after I'd hung up. "Your presence is required by Clovis, your mother."

"Come and eat with us, Sara Jo, please," Katie pleaded.

"No indeedy," I told her, feeling the words roll around in my mouth for a long time before I got them out straight. "I couldn't eat with Lily. Joleen doesn't even trust me enough to feed her by myself." I giggled.

After Katie left I began to feel supergood, so I finished her drink, too. Then I poured myself another just as the phone rang again.

"Wertzburger-Jacoby residence."

"Is that you, Sara Jo?" Mimi.

"It is I, and I want to thank you for asking."

"Do Joleen and Daniel know you answer the phone like that?"

"No, so don't tell them, okay? Joleen thinks I'm perfect."

"Stop being silly now. I'd like to speak to Joleen for a moment."

Mimi was probably getting nervous about the time. I could almost hear the dollar signs clicking in her eyes.

"*Everyone* would like to speak to Joleen, but the tragedy is that no one can. It is with great sadness —"

"Sara Jo! Put Joleen on this minute!"

"She's not home. Really. Joleen is on an errand of mercy. I believe she is praying for the soul of some poor alcoholic. I kid you not, Aunt Mimi."

"What's the matter with you tonight, young lady?"

"I'm just high on life, Aunt Mimi, that's all."

"Well, keep this in mind: I'd like to have one decent conversation with you before this summer is over. And please don't forget to tell Joleen to call me. Have you got that, Sara Jo?"

"Right on, Mimi," I said, and then I hung up quickly before the squawks began.

After that happy conversation I decided to have another martini, and then one more until all that booze finally made me sleepy. I wasn't thinking about how I looked anymore. I wasn't even aware that I had a head. When I got up to go upstairs the kitchen suddenly tilted on me, and without any warning, I vomited all over the table. That's when Joleen came in, with Lily trailing behind her. She took one look at me, and then she ran over and grabbed yards of paper towel from the holder over the sink.

"Sit down, honey." She put a cool cloth against my forehead and got to work cleaning up the table. But before I could get my breath, I had to jump up and run into the small john off the kitchen. And not a minute too soon, either.

Joleen came in after me with another wet towel and a glass of water.

"I think I'm okay now," I told her.

"Are you sure?" Joleen asked.

"I am, sir," I said, and giggled.

Joleen looked suspicious. "What's wrong with you, Sara?"

"I'm fine. If I felt any better, I'd be dead," I told her. "I'm sensational!"

That was when she walked over to the pitcher on the counter and sniffed inside it. Then she noticed the liquor bottles.

"You've been *drinking*? You made yourself martinis? Oh, Sara Jo." She sat down, shaking her head.

"You know what, Joleen, it works. I am feeling no pain. I don't hurt anymore. The corkscrews on my head don't hurt anymore. The color of my hair doesn't hurt anymore. Nothing hurts anymore! Everything is perfecto!"

"I know, darling," she said, and as she reached out to touch my arm, her hand trembled.

"This is the most super stuff. I think maybe I'll convert and become —" But I didn't finish. I had to run into the bathroom again.

This part was turning out not to be much fun. Well, so long as it didn't last for too long . . .

But it lasted forever. At two in the morning, Joleen found me draped over the john in the bathroom. I didn't have the energy to get up.

"I'm not going back to bed," I told her. "I don't stay there long enough to make the trip worthwhile."

"The gin's revenge," she said. "How's your headache?"

It was a jackhammer inside my brain and bones. "It's rotten."

A few minutes later she came back with Tylenol and tea. I shook my head. "I don't think so," I said. The tablets looked as big as baseballs, and the tea kept spinning around in its cup.

I finally fell asleep around five, but I was awake again at eight, so I put on my robe and went downstairs for some sympathy. My headache was gone, my stomach was quiet, but I felt awful anyway.

Daniel was just finishing his breakfast, and Joleen looked up from buttering a roll for Lily, who was coming toward me with her sticky fingers spread out. "Sar-ry! Sar-ry!"

Oh, please don't do that. Lily's voice had started my head pounding again, and I could almost feel it rolling around in my stomach.

"You're very pale, Sara," Daniel said. "You might feel better if you had a little juice and toast." Was he frowning at me, or at something else?

"I couldn't," I said, sitting down because the floor had begun to heave.

"I didn't give you anything to stop your vomiting last night because you needed to get the alcohol out of your system, and also because your mother and I decided that you might as well have the whole experience of one good drunk. You know, there's no absolute medical proof, Sara Jo, but because your mother is an alcoholic, you have to be a lot more careful than the ordinary social drinker. You're much more susceptible to the disease." I was dying and he was reading a textbook to me.

They were both creeps. But right then all I wanted to do was crawl back into bed.

Joleen was looking at me so I spoke to her. "Can you recommend anything good for a hangover?"

"Time," she said, sounding indifferent.

"How come you don't even care how I feel?" I asked her, my voice teary.

"I do care how you feel, Sara Jo. And I know you feel just awful right now, but I also know you'll get over it. Some day soon you're going to have to start being responsible for the things you do," she said.

Daniel left for the hospital then, and Joleen and I sat looking at each other.

"Why did you do it?" she asked.

"Because I couldn't stand the way I looked," I mumbled. What I didn't need then was to be put on trial.

Joleen looked upset. Her eyes were too bright, and for a moment I thought maybe there were tears in them.

"I drank for reasons like that," Joleen said, "because I couldn't be all the perfect things I thought your father wanted me to be, because Mimi ran his house with such efficiency and I knew I could never do that. All kinds of reasons. I drank because I hurt, and I couldn't tell anybody about the pain."

"So? Did it work?"

"Sure it did. In the beginning. But by the end I didn't need any reasons and I couldn't stop."

Despite how awful I felt, I was kind of interested.

"You couldn't, or you just didn't want to?" I asked her.

She shook her head. "I couldn't. It's an addiction, Sara Jo. A disease. I fought it for years."

"But now you're cured, right?"

"I'm not cured," Joleen surprised me by saying. "I'm sort of in remission. That's why I go to AA. It's a support group, a help for me to be with other alcoholics who suffered the way I did. But if I picked up another drink, it would start all over again. It's like I'm allergic to alcohol. Do you understand what I'm saying, Sara?"

Oh sure I could understand what she was saying. I could even remember back to some of the stuff I'd read in the library, so things were falling into place. Until Joleen said "suffered." That word really got to me. It made me mad as hell.

"You're not the only one who had to suffer, you know," I told her.

"I know," she said quietly. "You did, too. That's why I wanted you to be here so much this summer, Sassy. I've missed you, I've missed so much of your growing —"

This was getting to be too much for me. I was feeling bad enough, and now Joleen was crowding in again; she was getting too close and she was scaring me.

"Well, now you get another chance," I said. "You get to watch Lily grow up instead. And I didn't even kill her on you, so you still have that privilege."

"I never thought you tried to kill Lily. I never thought that for a minute, Sassy honey."

"Will you stop calling me that damn name!" I jumped up, shaking. "And if you never thought so, how come you wouldn't even let me take care of her yesterday? How come you had to rush her off to stay with Clovis? You don't trust me, so why are you lying?"

"That's not true. I do trust you."

"Bullshit!"

"I don't like your language, Sara Jo," she said wearily, and

I could see all the warmth fading out her eyes. I was ruining everything, but I didn't know how to stop.

"Bullshit on that too," I said, pushing as far as I could.

"Fine," Joleen nodded. "Now you have some idea why I couldn't leave Lily with you. You're not responsible, Sara. You're talking like a child right now, and yesterday you acted like one. You don't leave a child in the care of another child." Her voice was as cold as steel.

I didn't say anything for a moment, and then I moved close to Joleen.

"I hate you," I told her. "I really do." And then, without flinching, she slapped me, hard, right across the face. I just stood there, looking at her for a minute, and then I turned around and walked upstairs.

So many times, things would start being more normal between Joleen and me, and then suddenly they'd sizzle up and fall apart. Was it my fault or hers? I didn't know. All I knew was that I felt miserable, and I was afraid that feeling would never go away.

Chapter Eight

About a week later, Taffy called to see if I wanted to go shopping with her and Katie. How come she was paying attention to me? I wasn't in her league, and that was fine with me.

"Shopping for what?"

"Just for clothes. We're going to Strawberries." Of course for clothes. Taffy wasn't exactly majoring in the classics.

I didn't have anything to do, and if I stayed around here, Joleen would probably want me to play in the little turtle pool with Lily. Besides, Katie would be going, too.

"Okay, I'll go," I told her.

Joleen was doing something at the sink, but she'd overheard my conversation.

"Are you going out, Sara Jo?"

"Shopping. To Strawberries." I was trying to keep everything brief with Joleen these days.

"Oh, that's good. Do you have enough money?"

"Sure," I told her. I didn't want Joleen to give me anything, and besides I hadn't spent much since I'd been here.

She picked Lily up in her arms. "Come on, baby, we'll get

our bathing suits on and see if Aunt Clovis will let us swim in her pool."

Aunt Clovis?

Just then Katie banged at the back door.

"Sara Jo?" she shaded her eyes. "Come on, Taffy can't wait to help us pick out some gen-u-ine sexy stuff."

"What?"

"Only kidding, don't get excited," Katie said. "Except my mother did tell me I should pay attention to any suggestions Taffy has. 'She has a lovely sense of color, dear.' That's what she said." Katie crossed her eyes at me.

I looked at Joleen, wondering if she was going to offer me any "motherly" advice, but she had her back to us, kneeling on the floor so Lily could climb up on her and play papoose. A little voice inside me was busy whispering that it wouldn't be totally awful if Joleen had some suggestions to make. She had a terrific sense of what went well with what, and I wasn't used to buying my own clothes. For a moment I hesitated, wanting to ask her if she had any thoughts about what wouldn't look too horrible with my weird hair, but then I chickened out.

"Are you ready?" Katie was getting impatient. "Taffy gets into a snit when you keep her waiting."

"Okay, okay," I said. "We certainly wouldn't want to ruffle any of your cousin's lovely feathers, right?"

Joleen laughed, and for some reason that made me feel good. "Have a good time," she called to us.

"Your mom is really neatsy," Katie said as we walked down the driveway to meet Taffy.

"How come I keep hearing this from you, Katie?"

93

"I don't know." Katie shrugged, and then she stopped and looked at me. "Aren't you having a good time this summer Sara Jo? Aren't you glad you're here?"

It was a hard question, and I didn't really want to think about it because when I did I felt kind of afraid about everything. If I started to like Joleen, if I started to care, wouldn't she just collapse on me again, like a house of cards?

"Come on, Katie," I said, grabbing her hand. "You don't want Taf to melt out in the sun, do you?"

I bought a dress. It was a very unusual dress, but I fell in love with it. A hand-painted cotton, pearl pink and white, with large swans floating all over it.

When I came out of the dressing room, I swirled around shyly for Katie and Taffy. I was afraid Taffy was going to laugh at me. Pink? Swans? Even though she was an airhead, she had lots of things I didn't have. I hated to admit it to myself, but I kind of wanted her to think I looked good.

"It's perfect!" Katie squealed. "You look great!"

"Very nice," Taffy said. Was that supposed to be a compliment?

Our next stop was the makeup counter, and I was surprised when Taffy handed me a pale coral lipstick and said, "This color would look good on you, Sara Jo. Why don't you buy it? And you ought to get yourself some blush and a light-colored base." She looked at me thoughtfully, as if I were a problem she was trying to solve. "You really have terrific skin," she finally said, and then she moved off down the counter. I did? No one had ever said that to me before, and for a dumb moment I just felt happy.

Then Katie took the lipstick out of my hand and read the bottom of it. "I don't believe it! Do you know what this lipstick is called? 'Kiss Me Coral'! Do you believe it, Sara Jo?" She puckered her face up at me. "Oh, kiss me, kiss me coral, Sara, please!"

"Give me that," I said, taking the tube away from her. "I want to look for some makeup base."

"Oh sure. For your 'terrific' skin, right?" Katie was getting annoyed.

"You'll understand when you get a little older," I told her coolly.

"I certainly hope not." Katie sounded so dignified, and so much like a miniature Clovis that I started to laugh.

While I was choosing the makeup, Taffy drifted over and made some suggestions that the saleswoman agreed with, and I decided to take a chance that they were both right. By that time, Katie was fuming at us.

"I'm bored," she said, "and I'm dying of starvation if anyone cares."

"Remind me not to go shopping with you again," Taffy told her.

"I will," Katie shot back. "Don't worry about it." And then she appealed to me. "Sara Jo, don't you want to at least eat something? I can't stand up on my legs anymore."

"I've still got some shopping I want to do," I told her, hoping my money was going to stretch a little further.

"*Now* what do you want to get?"

"You'll see," I said mysteriously. "Why don't you go up to the coffee shop and I'll meet you there."

"Sounds good to me." Katie looked a little brighter. "I'm in need of a hot fudge nut sundae with butterscotch sauce and marshmallows."

Taffy rolled her eyes to the ceiling. "You'll have zits all over your face if you eat like that."

"What do I care?" Katie asked her. "I like zits. They give you something to pick at when you can't fall asleep at night."

Taffy shuddered, and I left the two of them and headed for the bathing suit department, feeling very daring.

I did it. I bought a bikini. I only had one bathing suit and it was awful. A woolly black one-piece with a green silk butterfly stitched to the side of it. Naturally, Mimi had picked it out for me. That seemed like a very long time ago, and I wondered now why I had let her do it. Because you didn't care, I told myself, but now you do.

I put on a tiny chocolate brown suit and looked into the mirror. I looked good in it. I really did. Like I had a body for the first time in my life, or maybe it was just that I was noticing it for the first time. Then I took the top off and stood there looking at my breasts. It wasn't my imagination, they were definitely growing and getting fuller.

When I got to the coffee shop, Katie had a funny look on her face and Taffy seemed annoyed.

"What's with you two?" I asked them.

"My cousin just got this wonderfully dumb idea," Katie said. She had another chocolate mustache on her upper lip.

"What?" I slid into the booth and thought about having a sundae too. The remains of Katie's looked wonderful. But then I thought about zits and a soft, fleshy bulge popping up over my new bikini, and I knew I'd better not do it.

"I'll have an English muffin and black coffee," I told the waitress while Katie looked at me as if I'd just landed from outer space.

"What's the idea?" I asked again, before Katie could make any comments.

"Taffy wants to fix you up on a date. Isn't that cute? Isn't that just too too de-vine?" She scooped the remaining syrup from her dish and sucked it up noisily.

" 'Fix me up'? With who?" I was starting to feel pretty uncomfortable.

"You know Hank-the-Hunk that she goes out with?" Katie asked.

"Why don't you let me tell her, Junior," Taffy said.

"Sure." Katie sat back. "You tell her. She's going to be just thrilled."

"You know Hank?" Taffy said to me. "The guy I go with?"

I'd met him once. He was really good-looking. The kind of guy who always made me start mumbling and bumping into myself if I had to talk to him.

"I know Hank," I said, swallowing.

"Well, he has this younger brother —"

"Whose name is Hunky-dory the Second," Katie said, giggling because she thought that was a riot.

"Whose name is L.T." Taffy wasn't paying any attention to Katie now. "He's real sweet."

"How do you know that?" Katie demanded as I burned my mouth on my first gulp of coffee.

"Because I've met him," Taffy replied indignantly.

I was definitely getting nervous now, and all I could do

was look down at the butter glazing over the muffin I no longer wanted.

"L.T. needs a date for this church dance, I think it is, on Friday —"

"How come he can't find his own date?" I interrupted Taffy.

"Of course he can find his own date," she said, looking as if I'd insulted something about Hank. "But Hank said that when he told L.T. about you —"

"About me? What did he tell him about me? I don't even know Hank. I just met him once."

Taffy grinned. "So? Maybe once was enough. That's how it is with men," she said knowingly, "they know right away."

What did they know? What?

"Anyhow," Taffy continued, "I guess he described you to L.T., and now L.T. wants to take you out. Isn't that great?"

I wasn't sure what it was, but for some reason I decided right then that I wanted to find out. Besides, I had a new dress with swans floating all over it.

"Okay," I said, "I'll do it," and I heard Katie gag.

When we got back I took a shower and changed in Katie's bathroom. It was too hot to do anything but stay underwater for the rest of the day, and I was trying hard not to think about Friday and whoever this L.T. was going to turn out to be.

When I walked out to the pool in my new bikini I felt self-conscious, and Katie didn't help by yelling, "Sara Jo, you're naked!"

"I am not," I said, pulling at the top of my suit to make sure it was going to stay up.

Katie jumped into the pool and began to splash around. "Come on in," she said, "or are you afraid you're going to lose that little piece of material that's covering up your chest?"

"Of course I'm not." I sat down on the side of the pool and dangled my legs into the water.

"Then what are you waiting for?" Katie asked, floating over near me.

"I'm waiting because I'm afraid I'm going to lose the little piece of material that's covering up my chest!" I told her, and we both burst out laughing.

Then she gave my foot a tug. "Don't worry, you won't," she said. "Gosh, Sara Jo, I didn't even realize it, but you really have boobs, you know?"

I slipped into the water, feeling like a dope because Katie had made me blush. "You get at least ten Delaneys for that one," I told her, slapping water into her face.

"For what one? What did I say? Huh?"

" 'Boobs,' you boob," I said. "I'm sure, in Delaney language, that's considered a dirty word." By that time we were both feeling pretty good.

When I got home, Joleen was dropping cookie dough from a spoon onto a tin sheet.

"Did you have a good time?" she asked, licking her fingers, but she didn't look at me.

Ever since the slap we'd been very careful of each other, and right then Joleen appeared to be fascinated by the bits of glazed sugar she was sprinkling over the cookies.

"I bought a dress," I said.

"You also bought a bikini."

I didn't realize that she'd noticed, but she was smiling as if she liked the way I looked.

"It's, ah — called chocolate brown." I couldn't think of anything else to say.

"I can see that."

Evidently, neither could she.

"You look sensational," Katie said. She was bouncing around on my bed, supposedly helping me get ready.

"Are you sure?"

"I am more than positive," she told me. "L.T. is going to ravish you on sight."

"And what do you know about ravishing?"

"About as much as you do, probably," she said smartly.

That put us both close to zero.

It took me forty-five minutes to get ready, particularly because of my hair. I experimented by parting it in the center, and then combing it down tight on both sides. I dug tortoise-shell combs into each side, and curls sprung up all around them. I really thought it looked good, and so did Katie.

"You'd better hurry up, Sara Jo," she said. "He'll be here any minute, and your mom said she wanted to see how you look."

I'd forgotten about Joleen. She was in the dining room, polishing silver.

"Sara Jo." She just looked at me for a moment. "You are perfection. Oh, I wish Daniel were here," she said.

I smiled at her, and the feel of it made me wonder if I'd ever smiled at Joleen before.

And then the front chimes rang, and my heart began to gallop.

Joleen disappeared, and Katie giggled.

"Oh, God," I said, rushing for the front door. But halfway there, I turned back.

"Do you know how old he is?" I asked her, desperately wanting some kind of clue before I opened the door.

"Thirty-two." Katie whooped as the chimes rang again.

"Go home, L.T.," I whispered just before I opened the front door.

L.T. was waiting on the other side of it, but I was so nervous, I couldn't even see what he looked like.

"Hi, L.T. Would you like to come in?"

"What?"

Then I did look at him. He had a lot of brown hair hanging over his forehead, and he wore wire-rimmed glasses.

"I said, would you like to come in?"

"What for?" he asked.

"I don't know what for, I was just being polite."

"I think we'd better get going if we don't want to be late." He turned and started down the walk without me.

"Hey, you forgot something," I called after him, and then he stopped to wait for me. "Thanks a lot," I said.

"Listen, do you really want to go to this dance, Sara Jo?" he asked, as we walked down the street toward the bus stop.

"Why? Don't you?" I wondered who'd given L.T. initials for a nickname. Initials belonged strictly to jocks, as far as I was concerned.

He turned and looked at me. "Let's do something else, all right?"

"Why?"

"I hate dances."

"Then why did you ask me to go to this one?"

"Because of Hank, I guess."

"And what did Hank do, crush your bones?"

L.T. looked embarrassed. "Actually, Hank just told me you were terrific, and I tried to think of something we could do. I guess maybe I made a mistake about the dance."

We stood there, looking down at each other's feet. I didn't want to just go home. That would be humiliating. And we couldn't walk around or drink Cokes all night, either.

"Do you want to go to the movies?" I finally asked him.

"Okay, if you want to."

And then I got mad.

"L.T.? You know, you're not exactly turning me on. You ask me to a dance you don't want to go to. Then I suggest a movie, and you practically fall asleep on your feet. You're not winning me over, you know that?"

"Hey, wait. Don't get mad, Sara Jo." He really sounded concerned. "I want to take you to the movies, really."

So we went to see a revival of Bette Midler in *The Rose*. Dynamite stuff. But L.T. kept fidgeting, and about halfway through the movie he put his arm on the back of my seat. I could see him trying to peer at me through the darkness.

"Do you want to hold hands?" he whispered.

"No!"

"All right, don't have a seizure over it." He was annoyed.

I leaned toward him and asked, "What made you think I'd hold hands with you?" I was really curious.

"I didn't think you would, I just wanted you to, that's all," he said.

He smelled of peppermint, and I wondered if that's the way boys smelled, or was it just L.T.? Would I ever know secret things about boys, the way Taffy did? Like how their skin felt right after they shaved, or why they always talked so tough and had to smack each other around?

L.T. tapped my shoulder just as the finale began.

"You want to leave now so we don't get trampled? We can stop for a soda or something."

"Sure." I was glad he wasn't going to take me home right away. I wanted to practice being with L.T.

We sat at a back booth in The Soda Shoppe, and we both ordered double malts and burgers.

I looked around, and there were five or six other couples, all older than we were. And were they involved with each other! You could just see it. The girls all looked like Needlewood girls, only they wore even more makeup. This one girl kept touching the guy she was with. His arm, his fingers, the tip of his nose. I thought she was disgusting, but I couldn't stop looking at her.

"Why are you squinting like that?" L.T. asked me.

"I've been watching that girl over there."

"Yeah? So?"

"I was just observing," I told him coldly, and then I picked up my purse and stood up. This whole boy-girl scene was making me nervous. "I'd like to go home," I said.

"But they haven't brought our food yet!"

L.T. slapped some money down on the table and told the

girl who was touching her boyfriend that she could have our order, but I don't think she heard him.

When we got to Joleen's, he stopped under the light from the fan-shaped window above the door.

I took my key out and jingled it. Was I supposed to thank him? A moth was beating at the glass overhead, and I could smell L.T.'s cologne again. I leaned against the door and watched him take his glasses off. There was a June bug crawling on the flagstone, and when I looked at L.T. again, I smiled. His eyes were nice. It was amazing how different his face was without glasses. All of a sudden, I wished we had waited for our food. I heard a breeze rush through the leaves of the weeping birch in the yard.

"Did you ever see a weeping birch?" I asked L.T.

He shook his head, and we walked over to it through the grass. L.T. put his hand on my shoulder, and my heart started to pound.

"You're pretty, Sara Jo."

His voice was low and different.

He put one hand on my waist, and I trembled. Then he lifted my face, and I closed my eyes as he kissed me. It was lovely. But all of a sudden a light went on in a bedroom upstairs, and I jumped.

I moved away from L.T., but I kept looking at his lips. I wanted him to kiss me again.

We walked back through the grass to the front door. I still had my key in my hand.

"Good night, Sara Jo," L.T. said.

"Good night, L.T."

Chapter Nine

"Sara Jo, it's L.T." Joleen called upstairs, where I was getting a pile of laundry together.

I ran to the extension.

"Hello?"

"Hi, Sara Jo, what're you doing?"

"Counting the freckles on my arm." I never know how to answer questions like that. I'm not usually doing anything interesting enough to talk about.

"Yeah? What number are you on?"

I smiled. Not bad. How come he hadn't been funny like this last night?

"So, how about it? You want to see another flick with me?"

"What does L.T. stand for?" I asked him, sitting down on Joleen and Daniel's bed.

"Lawrence Tremain, and before you ask, Tremain is a family name."

"It's nice." But then I thought about calling him Tremain, and I giggled.

"Tremain really turns you on, huh?"

"How old are you, L.T.?" I was enjoying myself.

"What is this, an interview?" But he didn't sound mad.

He likes me, I thought.

"All right. I'm fifteen. Almost sixteen."

"Get out," I said. He couldn't be.

"Sara Jo." Now he was getting impatient. "Are we on?"

"For when?"

"How about tonight?"

"All right."

"Did you say yes?"

"Yes, I said yes," I told him, and then we talked for a few minutes more.

"Joleen?" I called down to her after I hung up.

"Sara Jo, dammit, don't call me that!" She came to the foot of the stairs with a sailor hat covering her hair, and a dust mop in her hand. "What is it?"

"I'm using the phone again, okay?"

"Yes, all right."

Great. I wanted to talk to Katie, even though I wasn't sure she'd understand about L.T. She was probably too young, but I was excited and I had to talk to someone. I thought about Joleen, and for a moment I was tempted. Something told me that she'd understand how good I was feeling. I had this instant picture of the two of us sitting together in my room and how maybe it would be nice to tell her about last night with L.T. . . . And then I heard her say, "Sara Jo, dammit, don't call me that!" and I knew it would never work. Did she really expect me to call her "Mother" or "Mom"? I couldn't do that. I wouldn't feel comfortable. But then there wasn't much I *was* comfortable about this summer.

I wasn't going to get into sharing mother-daughter confidences with Joleen (what else could I call her? Mrs. Wertzburger?), and I wasn't about to share anything with Taffy the space cadet, either. I had crossed Mimi off my list. So that left Katie. It was maybe a little weird because of our ages, but she was probably the closest friend I'd had in years.

While I waited for her to come over I lay on my bed and thought about L.T. and the way I'd felt after he kissed me last night. I started to smile.

"Hey, are you grinning in your sleep, Sara Jo?" Katie jumped on the bed next to me.

"Take it easy," I said, "you're interfering with my fantasy life."

"Are you dreaming about L.T.? Are you in love with him?" Behind her thick glasses, Katie's eyes were shining and I felt like giving her a hug.

"Of course I'm not in love with him, you dope!" I picked up a pillow and tossed it at her. "But he's okay. I'm going out with him again tonight," I added nonchalantly.

"Oh." I heard the fizz go out of Katie's voice. "That's nice," she finally said, but I could tell that she didn't think that it was.

"What's the matter?" I sat up and looked at her.

"Nothing. What could be the matter? You have a boyfriend, and my mother and I just got back from trotting me into town so I could enroll in charm school for the fall."

"Well, I think you're charming enough right now, Katie."

"Would you quit making fun of me, Sara Jo?"

"I'm not making fun of you."

"You think you're so grown up right now, you know? Big deal, so you're going out with L.T. You're still practically only a kid. You're hardly any older than I am."

"So?" I was getting angry.

"So now all you can talk about is all this other junk. My date, my period, my dress, my hair," she mimicked. "I mean you only just graduated from junior high, Sara Jo!"

"Will you quit attacking me, Katie? Things change, you know? And I don't owe you any explanations. If you don't understand, too bad, but you'd do me a favor if you could stop acting like a little creep."

Damn. I hadn't meant to say that. I knew Katie was just feeling left out, and that she was probably kind of jealous too. I remembered how I had felt with the kids in Boston.

"Katie —" But she'd already gone.

"Have you and Katie been playing hopscotch on your bed?" Joleen stood in the doorway with a cleaning bucket in her hand.

"Sorry." I jumped up and straightened the comforter.

"Why did Katie go running out of here so fast?"

"Her feelings got hurt," I said, pulling at the pillows.

"Does that mean you hurt them?" She tugged at a few corners until the bed was straight.

"Who *else* could have hurt them? I was the only person here, wasn't I?" I was feeling bad and I didn't want Mrs. Wertzburger on my case.

Joleen sighed. "You can really be rude, Sara Jo. Okay,

what did L.T. want? Did you have a good time last night?"

"It was okay. He wanted me to go out with him again tonight."

"What did you tell him?"

"I told him I was hot to trot," I said.

"You always have to try and stamp on every conversation we have, don't you?" she asked angrily.

"*I* stamp? That's crazy. You're the one who puts your big cleats on and —"

Joleen held up her hand. "All right, that's enough. I've heard enough for one day, and right now *I* need a little space." She walked to the door and then turned back. "On Monday, I'm going into the hospital. Clovis will take Lily until Daniel gets home. There'll be enough food in the freezer, and if there's anything else you need, the Delaneys will probably have it."

"Why are you going to the hospital?"

"For minor surgery, no big deal," she said, and went downstairs.

Joleen was at a meeting but Daniel was home when L.T. arrived. We talked for a few awkward minutes, and then Daniel came into the living room, carrying his newspaper.

"Where are you two going?" he asked.

"We're going to see a movie," L.T. said.

Daniel turned to me. "Did Joleen tell you what time to be home, Sara Jo?"

"No, she didn't."

"Well," he turned to L.T., "what time is the show over?"

L.T. shrugged.

"Eleven," I said.

"How about twelve then? No later." He gave my shoulder a little hug, and I stiffened up. I still wasn't used to being touched, and this was a very touchy-feely household.

"Is that your father?" L.T. asked when we were outside.

"No. He's supposed to be my stepfather," I told him.

"What do you mean 'supposed to be'?"

L.T. was totally different. Not at all like last night when he kissed me.

"Look, L.T., my family life is too complicated to go into."

By the time we'd taken the bus to the movies and L.T. had bought the tickets, I was sorry I'd come.

He reached for my hand as soon as we sat down, and I let him hold it. Maybe some of the magic would come back. But after a while my fingers got numb, and I pulled away from him.

"What's the matter?" L.T. whispered.

"My hand's asleep," I whispered back.

"Oh."

He put his arm around my shoulders, and when I felt his fingers on my skin, I began to feel a little better about L.T. He was sort of stroking my arm, and I wondered if I'd let him kiss me again.

I put a gumdrop into my mouth and decided that I would let L.T. kiss me if he wanted to. I was pretty sure he'd want to, and I started looking forward to it. I thought kissing was probably the nicest experience I'd ever had.

110

When the movie was over we walked up Main Street holding hands.

"Do you want to get a chocolate Coke?" I asked him.

"All right, we'll get them to go," he said.

"To go where?"

"Isn't there a bandstand at the end of this block?" he asked me. "With a little park?"

"Listen, L.T. —"

"Hey, Sara, don't you trust me?"

"No," I said, but then I felt silly.

By the time we got to the bandstand with our Cokes I'd stopped being nervous. L.T. and I sat down on the grass.

"Sara?"

"What?" He picked up my hand and held it in both of his.

"Do you like me, Sara?"

"I like you," I told him.

"Me too. I like you a lot."

And then we didn't say anything for a while, till L.T. put his hand on the back of my neck. "Can I kiss you now?"

I turned my face and we kissed. L.T. put his arms around me and held me close to him. It was lovely.

We walked back to Joleen's holding hands, and when we got to the door, he kissed me again, and that was wonderful too.

When I got in there was a note propped up on the kitchen table for me.

"You want to come over for a pajama party? I'll let you talk about L.T. The side door is unlocked, and I'll be waiting up for you, okay? Katie."

Terrific! I was too excited to sleep anyway. I left Joleen a note and went upstairs for my toothbrush and nightshirt.

Inside the Delaneys' it was very dark, and it took me a long time to feel my way to Katie's room. When I got there I tapped softly on the door.

"It's me," I whispered.

Katie opened the door a crack. "You don't have L.T. with you, do you?"

"Katie, are you crazy?!"

"Well, all of a sudden, I just thought maybe —"

"Can I come in? You did invite me, right?" I hissed as loudly as I dared.

"All right, all right, don't wake the whole house up!" Katie opened the door.

"I thought you were going to be a little friendlier," I said.

"I am friendly! I'm probably the friendliest person you're ever going to meet." She gave me a wide phony grin that reached from one ear to the other. "So did you have a good time tonight?"

"I had a great time." If Katie was willing to try then I certainly was too.

She gave me a strange look. "Is there something different about you, Sara Jo? You look kind of weird."

"I am different. Tonight I am a woman!" I started to giggle.

"And what is that supposed to mean?" She narrowed her eyes at me suspiciously.

Then, as I got into my nightshirt, I told Katie almost everything. That L.T. and I had kissed under the weeping birch, and how it felt. And then about tonight, when I didn't

112

like him at all in the beginning, and how it got different. I was dying to share my feelings with someone.

"I wanted him to keep kissing me all night, Katie. I didn't want him to stop."

Katie looked upset. "What do you mean, you didn't want him to stop? What did you want him to do?" Her voice sounded funny.

"I don't know. It was just the way I felt. I guess I didn't want it to stop because it felt so good. You know what, Katie? He said I was sexy. Isn't that incredible?"

"*Sexy*? Did he really tell you that?" Katie was yanking at her braid as if she meant to pull it off.

"Yes," I said dreamily. "He made me feel beautiful. Oh, Katie, wait till you feel like this. Wow."

"I can wait," Katie said. "I can wait forever. Yuck."

"What do you mean, 'yuck'?" I was hurt.

"Just yuck, Sara Jo. All that kissing stuff. It's like you've been reading dirty magazines or something. Is that all you can think about? I don't believe all this."

"You don't understand," I told her, feeling awful. I almost wished I could talk to Taffy. Someone, anyone, who would know what I was talking about.

The only reason I decided to stay at the Delaneys' all night was that I didn't feel like facing another trip out into the dark again, and sneaking through two houses.

I made myself yawn a big wide, exaggerated yawn. "Let's go to sleep," I said. "I can't keep my eyes open."

"That's fine with me." Katie flounced around, tugging the spreads off the beds and shaking her head at me like a maiden aunt.

*

By the time I got to Joleen's the next morning I was in a rotten mood. Katie wasn't talking to me, and I didn't know when I was going to see L.T. again. So when I walked into the kitchen and saw Joleen practically tapping her foot at me, I decided I'd just say hi and go straight to my room. But it didn't work.

"Sara Jo, please don't rush away."

I dropped my tote bag and turned around.

"I assume you spent the night with Katie? Common courtesy might have told you to leave us a note." Her tone was pure frost.

"I *left* you a note," I told her. "I propped it up on the saltcellar, right on the counter you're leaning against."

"All right," Joleen said tiredly, but I didn't think she believed me.

"You had a phone call," Joleen said. "It was your friend L.T. You're supposed to call him back."

"Okay."

"He was very rude over the phone."

"Why? What did he say?"

All I needed was to lose L.T. now.

"He said, 'Put Sara Jo on, please.' That's what he said."

"So? He said 'please,' didn't he?"

"Sara Jo, I don't want you to see L.T. until I get back from the hospital. Then we can have him over for dinner if you want."

Okay, Joleen. One push too many. "I don't believe this!" I exploded. "If I want to see L.T. it's none of your damn —"

"Stop right there, Sara Jo." Daniel was standing in the

114

doorway, looking like a thundercloud. "Never," his voice bounced off the kitchen cabinets, "never let me hear you speak like that to your mother again! Is that understood?" He waited. "Well, is it?"

I nodded.

"All right, go upstairs to your room now," he said, dismissing me.

And my room is where I stayed until I heard them get Lily and back the car out of the garage. Then I went downstairs and called L.T.

"Couldn't you have been a little bit polite to Joleen?" I asked him.

"Who is this, please?" he said.

"You're not funny, L.T."

"Is this the sexpot of Locust Valley?"

"L.T., stop it!"

"When are you going to go out with me again, Sara?" he asked.

I sighed right into the phone.

"That doesn't sound very good."

"Listen, we have to kind of cool it for a while," I told him.

"What do you mean 'cool it'? Are you mad at me?"

"No, I'm not mad. It's just that my — my family thinks that two nights in a row is too much. And they'd like to meet you. To talk and all," I said.

"Ah, I get it. You had the screws applied, right?"

"I guess so."

"Well, okay. I'll drop around and chat for a while. They'll like me. I'll be charming. You have nothing to worry about, Sara Jo."

"No, you can't do that, L.T. Or at least you can't do that now," I said.

"Then when can I do it?"

"Well, could you call me next week? Maybe I'll know better then," I told him.

"Sara?"

"What?" The way his voice sounded made goose skin spring up on my arms.

"I really like kissing you, you know?"

"That's good." I didn't know what to say. Too many things were happening at once and I was a little shaky.

"Hey, you're not mad, are you?" he said.

"No," I told him, "I just feel kind of rotten today."

"Listen, I'll call you soon."

"Thanks, L.T." I hung up.

We had dinner a little while after the three of them got home, and we all carried white peace flags with us. Afterward, we sat around the kitchen table eating peaches, and that's when I asked Joleen what a little minor surgery meant.

It took her a while to answer. As if she were trying to make up her mind about something. And then she looked straight at me, and I thought she was going to cry.

"I'll try to explain, Sara Jo," she finally managed to say. "Daniel and I had planned on having four children. That's how many we both wanted. Four, counting Lily and you. But that's not going to be possible now because I have to have an operation. I won't be able to have any more . . . any more . . ." The tears were dripping down Joleen's face, and Daniel took her hand.

I didn't know what to say, but I saw how upset Joleen was,

and I really felt bad. "I'm sorry," I told her. After a few minutes I began to feel very uncomfortable, as if I were intruding on the two of them. I thought they wanted to be alone together.

"I'm going to call Katie and see if she wants to swim," I said, and when neither of them answered, I went upstairs.

Of course, Clovis answered.

"How are you, Sara Jo, dear?"

"Oh, I'm fine."

"Well, let me see if I can scare Katie up. But I think she's a little peeved at you, dear. Now don't you be upsetting our Katie," she brayed into the phone.

Katie wasn't the only one who was upset. So far this day had been truly forgettable.

I waited for quite a while, and then I heard the receiver being picked up, but no one spoke. No one being Katie.

I waited some more, and then I said, "Katie, if this is to see who can hold out the longest, you just won."

"Big deal."

"Well, are you talking to me or not?"

"Well, are you going to start talking about all that stuff again or not?"

"Katie, I'm not. I'm down on my knees promising you, begging your forgiveness, all right? If you walked in here right now you'd swear you were in a church."

She tried to muffle the sound, but I could hear her giggling anyway.

"Do you want to go swimming? I'll bring you over a peach. It's red and cold and hairy. You'll love it."

"When are you coming over?"

"Twenty minutes," I said and hung up.

Today even the water in the indigo pool felt warm, and after floating around for a while, I got out and went to sit in the shade.

"You think it's cooler here?" Katie asked, pulling off her cap.

"I was hoping," I said, shaking the water out of my hair. The sunflower had a leak. "Wouldn't it be great to go skinny-dipping?" I asked her.

"Take off our bathing suits, you mean? Would you really do that, Sara Jo?"

"Yes," I said, thinking how nice it would feel.

"Sara Jo, how come you have breasts already?" I couldn't believe she was asking me that.

"Katie." I looked straight at her. "How much do you really know?"

"About all that stuff?"

"Yeah," I told her, "about all that stuff."

"I know everything. Clovis drew me this diagram. She told me it was a very 'meaningful' diagram. It's where this X goes into this Y and a little O is born."

"Well, that makes it all totally clear."

"So?" she asked, sticking her flat chest out at me. "When am I going to get them, do you think?"

"Katie, I'm a lot older than you are."

"A lot?" She made a face at me. "You're not a *lot*."

"I am, skinny-bones."

"And stop calling me stupid things."

"Taffy has breasts," I said to distract her.

"Taffy?" she hooted. "Taffy is *huge*, not like you!"

118

"Okay, Katie, that's enough," I said.

"Don't get mad, Sara Jo. I just meant that Taffy is top-heavy."

I thought it was time to change the subject.

"Katie, how come you told Clovis I upset you?"

"Oh, I was crying before and she got nosy, that's all." I wondered how much she'd said, but I was afraid to ask. Probably the less Katie and I discussed L.T., the happier we'd be.

"Hey, it's getting too hot," I said, "let's go back in the pool."

I tugged the sunflower on and dove in. The water was cooler now, and I floated around under the shade of the diving board until Katie bobbed up next to me.

"Are you really in love with L.T., Sara Jo?"

Why was she bringing him up again?

"You're impossible, do you know that?"

"Sure I do." She grinned.

Then I got evil. I was tired of Katie going hot and cold on me, and I was fed up with everything else too, so without thinking about it, I got out my double guns for a whammy.

"Can you keep a secret, Katie?"

"Of course I can keep a secret." She looked serious. "Do you know how many —"

"Okay, okay, I believe you," I told her, and then I gave Katie this really riveting look. "I didn't tell you before, but I'll tell you now. L.T. and I did more than just kiss last night. A lot more."

"What is that supposed to mean?" There were question marks popping out all over her, and she looked a little bit scared too. Then suddenly, I knew I couldn't do it. I didn't want to make up anything that happened between L.T. and me, and I wasn't being fair to Katie either. Why should I make up something to confuse her and hurt her just because I was feeling bad? Without wanting to, I remembered what Joleen had said about growing up and being responsible. I got mad at myself.

But Katie wasn't going to listen to anymore, anyway. Her eyes looked like two hard black rocks, and her mouth was tucked in at the corners. "Sara Jo, you must think I'm some kind of jerk if you think I believe you! You just want to make up a stupid big thing that never even happened anyway. I'm not dumb, you know? So please stop treating me that way!"

She had tears in her eyes, and I felt rotten.

"Katie?" I put my hand on her shoulder, but she ducked out from under me.

"I don't care if you're sorry, Sara Jo, so don't say it!"

Tears were running down her cheeks, but I didn't know what to do, except maybe leave. Yes, I could do that.

I swam over to the steps and climbed out of the pool.

"Katie, I'm sorry. Even if you don't want to hear it, I really am."

But I don't think she heard me. Even if she was listening.

My skin was goose bumps all the way back to Joleen's.

Chapter Ten

Joleen wouldn't be home till the end of the week, and all during that time I took care of Lily only once, while Clovis ran an errand. I was lonely and depressed those days, and it really helped that Lily liked me so much.

"Put Lily up! Put Lily up!" She pestered me, until I lifted her onto my shoulders and galloped around the house.

"Stairs!" she screamed, but I couldn't manage Lily and the stairs.

"You're too heavy," I told her.

"Lily be light now. Come on, Sarry!" She grabbed hold of my hair and tugged until I felt the roots quiver.

"Sarry's going to beat Lily up, you know that, Lily?" I swung her down and chased her into the kitchen, where she grabbed onto the refrigerator door, yelling and giggling.

And then Daniel came in the back door.

"The father is home," he sang. "Why isn't at least the little daughter running to give him a hug if the big one is too old for that stuff?" He bent down and opened his arms. Lily made a mad dash and landed on Daniel's chest, giggling and hugging. He threw her up into the air and caught her just before she came down. Lily was ecstatic.

"What smells so good?" Daniel asked me.

"Joleen made it. Peas and pasta," I told him.

"Do I have time to take a shower first?"

"Sure. I'll tie Lily up down here so you can have some privacy."

As soon as she heard "tie," Lily ran around the kitchen giving Indian whoops. Then she stopped with her hands stretched out in front of her and her wrists crossed.

"Get rope, Sarry! Get rope!"

"What's all this about?" Daniel stopped to watch us.

"Oh, I started a crazy game with her this afternoon. Lily is an Indian princess —"

"Ka-wa-tee-woo! Princess Kawateewoo!"

"Well, excuse me," Daniel told her.

"Yeah, you'd better watch yourself," I said.

"So what happens to the princess?" he asked.

"She die!" Lily told him darkly.

"And how does she die?" Daniel turned to me.

"So far I've just burned her at the stake," I told him. "Can you think of something better?"

"Well, let's see. You could tie her to a tree and shoot her through the heart with an arrow."

"Yeah! Get arrow, Sarry. Lily die!"

"You're a gruesome little kid, Lily," I told her, and then I turned to Daniel. "Do you have any arrows around?"

"I'm taking my shower," he said. "You two may be catching."

I fed Lily and put her in the jump seat while we ate, and at seven-thirty Daniel took her up and tucked her into bed.

Joleen had always made bedtimes special. I guess she did that even when she was drinking. She used to tell me wild stories — like the one about a dragon who ate nothing but onions, and belched so loudly that he caused an earthquake in his kingdom. And sometimes we'd play games she made up, like Tunnel, where we were caterpillars crawling under the bed and through the closets. I used to laugh so hard that my tummy ached. Then one night, Harry was passing my door, and he stopped and looked in. "She shouldn't be played with like that at bedtime, Joleen," he said. But she just shook her head and went back to being a bull who was going to gore me to death, shouting, "Olé, olé!"

"She fell asleep while I was carrying her upstairs." Daniel came into the kitchen, stifling a yawn.

"Joleen left a pitcher of watermelon punch in the refrigerator," I told him, making a face. "It's got everything in it but the seeds and the rind."

He took two glasses down from a cabinet. "Sara Jo, don't you ever have anything nice to say about your mother?" He didn't wait for me to answer. "Sit down and we'll talk."

I didn't exactly have twenty choices.

"I wasn't really mocking."

"Yes, you were."

I shrugged. "I don't know," I told him. "Joleen and I don't have anything in common —"

"She says you're very alike."

"Oh, yeah. We're mirror reflections of each other."

"You won't stop being angry, will you, Sara Jo?" he said.

"When all it's doing is hurting the hell out of you. It's an old anger, Sara, and you're going to feel better when you can shake it off."

Easy for you to say, I thought. It's so simple for people to see situations clearly when their own feelings aren't involved.

"The problem with anger, or with any other negative emotion," Daniel went on, "is that it makes the person who is going through it feel black and bitter inside."

Was that me he was describing?

Neither one of us said anything then, and when Daniel reached for his punch, he tipped the glass over.

"Men," I said, sopping up the spill.

"Men, hmm, Ms. Jacoby?"

I saw a whole lot of arrows pointing straight at L.T.

"Tell me about L.T."

"He's nice," I said, but I didn't say anything else.

"So you're not going to talk about your love life, huh?"

Okay, so he thought L.T. and I were two pretty funny kids. Fine. I could play the innocent young teenager.

"You're a clam," he said, mussing my hair.

I hadn't spoken to Katie since Sunday evening, and I still didn't know how to approach her. I was hoping we'd just bump into each other and that everything would be natural when we did. That was what I was hoping, but I doubted that it would happen.

On Thursday, I was shredding cabbage for cole slaw when the phone rang around noon. I hoped it was either Katie or L.T. But it was Mimi.

"Surprise, Sara," she said.

A voice from beyond. Mimi got further and further away all the time.

"What's new?" I asked her. "How's Thelma?"

"She's having a lot of problems with Heidi. That's her oldest," Mimi said.

"I know." Heidi is sixteen, and my guess is that she's been out walking the streets for at least two years.

"And how are things with you, Sara?"

"Fine," I told her. And I almost added, but I'll know a lot more after the pregnancy test results are in; unfortunately humor wasn't Mimi's strong suit.

"That's good. All right, now let me speak to Joleen, please."

Her buddy.

"She's not home."

"Still in the hospital?"

"Yes."

"Well, I just spoke to her yesterday . . ."

Ya-da-ta, ya-da-ta, ya-da-ta. Two hens clucking on a fence. I started to get angry. Joleen was even reporting on me from the hospital. I'd bet she told Mimi about L.T.

"Did you hear me, Sara Jo?"

"No, I'm sorry, I didn't."

"Well, please listen. This is important."

Then she told me the great news. She was going to be in New York tomorrow, so she would spend the night with us. I really didn't want to see Mimi, but I knew I didn't have any choice about it.

I'd just hung up when the door chimed.

Katie. This time it had to be Katie. But it was L.T. He was

wearing khaki shorts and a yellow T-shirt, and he was grinning.

"What are you doing here?" I asked him, but I wasn't mad.

"Let me in, lady," he said, "you're air-conditioning the whole neighborhood."

"How come you're here?" I asked again.

He lowered his voice. "To charm your family, okay?"

"Sure, but I'm the only member of my family that's here right now." It felt weird to say "my family," but I guess in a way that's what they were.

"Swell," L.T. said, "then we can charm each other."

"No, we can't. Let's go for a walk, L.T."

It was sizzling hot, and by the time we got to town all I could think about was having an icy soda.

Walking into The Soda Shoppe was like standing under a wonderful cold shower. L.T. and I sat at a little corner table and had three sodas apiece. Heaven.

On the way home, he held my hand.

"Are we going together, Sara Jo?" he asked me.

"I don't know, L.T.," I said, and I took my hand back. Everyone I met this summer wanted an instant relationship! In Boston, in the Jacoby household, we did things a lot more slowly.

"Why not?" He sounded hurt.

"L.T., we've only known each other since a week ago Friday."

"Really? Then that means tomorrow is our one-week anniversary, right? Okay, so I'm taking you out to dinner tomorrow."

"All right." It seemed to me that no one had ever been as nice to me as L.T. He cared so much that he made it easy for me to care back. I moved closer so I could put my head against his shoulder.

When we got to the house, the garage door was open and Daniel's car was there. L.T. wanted to come in with me, but I told him he couldn't.

"Joleen just got home from the hospital, and everything's probably crazy in there."

"Then I'll meet them tomorrow, right?"

"Right." I knew he wanted to kiss me, and I wanted him to, but there was no way we could. We were standing on the sidewalk in front of the house, and L.T. was holding my hand.

"Please come inside, Sara Jo," Daniel called from the doorway.

I started to get angry until I remembered that I wasn't supposed to see L.T. until they'd had a chance to look him over.

"I've got to go," I told him. My heart was racing. L.T. waved at Daniel, and Daniel gave him a half wave back.

I went straight into the living room. Joleen was sitting on the couch with Lily sprawled all over her; she didn't look too terrific, and I wanted to ask her how she felt, but I didn't get a chance.

"Sara Jo, what were you doing with L.T. just now?"

"We were motel hopping," I told her. What the hell did she think we were doing?

"You weren't supposed to see L.T., do you remember

that?" Daniel said, sitting down on the couch, too.

"I remember it now, but I didn't when he came over," I said.

Everyone was silent, even Lily was like a little corpse.

"I didn't do anything wrong," I told them, and I could hear tears in the back of my voice. "L.T. came over to say hi to both of you, because I told him how you felt." My face was burning and my hands were icy. "Why am I always sitting in front of a tribunal? How come I al——"

Joleen clapped her hands together. "Okay, everybody, no more drama." She sat forward and Lily slid to the floor. "Sara Jo?"

"Yes?"

"I'm still a little weak in the knees. Clovis sent over some beef stock and rice, and I'm going to have that and then take a nap. Will you give Lily a bath and read her some of *Pinocchio*? Skip the part about the hatchet and Jiminy Cricket because she cries too hard. Did you hear what I said, Lily? Sarry's going to do good things with you."

Lily came running over to me. "Tell Jiminy Cricket," she demanded.

I tickled behind her neck. "Lily be papoose for big fat Indian lady?" I asked her, and she ran around behind me so I could pick her up. "Hold on tight," I said, galloping her out of the room. But before we got to the stairs, I heard Joleen say, "Those two are the one good thing about me today," and I felt something warm and nice start up in me, only I didn't know whether I should trust it or not.

After I got Lily in bed and gave her a lot of kisses, I thought I'd go down and see about dinner. There was still one casserole in the freezer, and I'd already cut up things for a salad. When I was halfway down the back stairs, I heard low voices, so I tiptoed the rest of the way down.

"You can't possibly know, dearie, how bad I feel about all this."

It was Clovis, and she was whispering so loud that Katie could have heard her next door.

I decided to listen for a while.

"My Katie was in tears when I told her." Clovis sounded like she might be in tears herself.

"Clovis," Joleen was talking, "I don't understand what's happening. You think Sara Jo is a bad influence on Katie? How?"

"The problem is, Joleen, I can't really say how, because Katie has clammed up on me. But I do know that lately when my Katie has been with Sara Jo, she comes home either depressed, whiny, or in tears. And there's not a thing in the world I can do with her."

I was perspiring, and my stomach had started to roll around. It meant the indigo pool, but that wasn't anything next to Katie. And I didn't know how I could fix it. How could I promise that I'd never mock Katie or hurt her again? I hadn't meant to do any of those things in the first place.

Joleen was trying to understand. "So you want the relationship between Katie and Sara Jo ended? Is that right, Clovis?"

"Well, I wouldn't like to call it ended, not really."

Clovis sounded like she had something in her mouth. Her fingers, maybe? She was always biting at the skin around her nails.

129

"Well, really what then?" Joleen asked. I could tell that she was getting impatient.

"How about if we slooow things down a lot. What do you say?"

"I say I don't know what you're talking about," Joleen told her.

"I think we should urge things into a stop gradually, and then let them slowly start up again, maybe. How does that sound?"

I could just picture Clovis. Her eyes must have been darting around furiously, and she was probably popping her knuckles, too.

Joleen said, "Confusing."

"Yes, well." Clovis was thinking. "Maybe an *occasional* swim together, but no, definitely no outside outings for quite a while. I think we just need to do things very, very gently."

"You mean you tell Katie, and I tell Sara Jo that they can meet only at the pool, and then only once a week?" Joleen sounded tired, and suddenly I felt guilty for giving her this problem when she was feeling so rotten.

"That sounds good to me, Joleen."

Clovis Delaney was an ass.

I clumped down the last few stairs and swung the kitchen door open.

"I'm sorry," I said, "but I overheard your conversation, and if you don't mind, there's something I'd like to say."

"Go ahead," Joleen said quietly. She was probably praying that I wouldn't say anything awful to Clovis.

"Talk ahead, Sara Jo," Clovis said. "This is your house,

too." I thought about one of Katie's favorite words: *yuck*.

"I just want you to know, Mrs. Delaney, that I'm sorry if I hurt Katie. I guess I don't always remember how young she is. But don't worry, I won't be coming over for a while." Once a week would be worse than never at all. How did she think we could have a friendship on those terms? She was crazy. My heart was beating fast and I felt like screaming, but I wouldn't let Clovis see that.

"Well, let's not let 'a while' be too long. Katie will really miss you, Sara Jo. And I want to thank you for understanding, I really do."

When she left, I couldn't help grinning at Joleen even though I felt awful. "Clovis isn't dealing with a full deck," I said.

"That's for certain." She reached up and turned on the Tiffany light above us.

"Do you feel like talking about Katie?" she asked me, but I shook my head.

"I guess I feel silent."

"Are you hungry?"

"No, just thirsty," I told her.

"I'll pour us some juice." She filled two glasses.

"You feel terrible about Katie, huh?"

I nodded. "But it's my fault," I made myself say.

"That's the bugger. It usually is."

"Thanks," I told her, heavy on the sarcasm.

"That's not what I meant, Sara Jo," she explained quickly. "I wasn't blaming you about this thing with Katie. I was talking generally. We usually bring on the bad things that hap-

131

pen to us. That's the worst of it, when you're forced to look at yourself and say, 'I did this, I was responsible, I own it, and I made it happen.' "

Her voice was tight, with an edge to it, and when I looked at her I realized that she was talking about herself. And me. And I didn't know what to say.

Then Joleen shook her head, as if she were trying to clear it. "Too much for tonight," she said. "I'm exhausted." She got up, stretched, and touched my hair lightly; I didn't flinch. "Try not to be too upset, honey. Things have a way of working themselves out if you don't push them too hard."

I looked up at her in surprise.

She smiled at me. "Well, that's something I learned from my daughter this summer."

After she went to bed, I sat alone in the kitchen, thinking. I remembered some things I did right after Joleen left, things I had forgotten about until now.

I used to spend hours in the attic and in the basement too, looking for her things and for pictures of her. It seemed that overnight Harry had gotten rid of everything that belonged to Joleen, every trace of her. I never found anything, not even a snapshot. It was awful. I could still see myself, sitting up in that dirty old attic and crying into a pile of musty smelling blankets so that I wouldn't make any noise.

After that I got sick a lot and I started wetting my bed at night. At first Harry was furious. He told me that I was just having tantrums. But then he started to get worried about me, and he took me to a doctor, who prescribed some kind of pills that made me sleepy all the time.

Eventually I stopped the bed-wetting and my father thought

I was cured. Actually, I'd just turned in another direction. I began writing to Joleen. Even though I had nowhere to send the letters, that didn't stop me. While I wrote to her it was as if she were there near me, and that made me feel a little better. I wrote for months and months, but one day I just stopped. I had this whole pile of letters that filled two big boot boxes, stashed away in the back of my closet, and I remember telling myself, "She'll never read these, and she's never going to come back either."

I lugged out the boxes early one morning before anyone was up and hid them out in back with the trash. By noon that day they were gone, and that's when I finally made myself stop thinking about Joleen. She was mean and ugly, I decided, and I would never let her hurt me again, I promised myself. Never.

I started to cry all over again, thinking about that little girl who was me. Then I thought about Katie and I cried some more.

Sometimes life really sucks.

Chapter Eleven

When I woke up the next day, I felt truly low. The sky was black and rain was thrumming down on the roof. I knew I had to fill time, but doing what? Because I was feeling kind of mellow about Joleen I decided I'd better stay away from her until I had time to think it all out.

By the time I got out of the shower, I'd decided to spend the day in town. At least I could look around in the stores, and then maybe I'd go to a movie.

I put on jeans and an old green trench coat, and then grabbed a beat-up umbrella that got turned inside out while I was waiting for the bus. I was less than glamorous, but after poking around in Strawberries for a while I thought maybe I'd feel better if I looked better. I browsed in the junior department where I decided I felt like looking funky today, but the problem was that I was kind of broke. Eventually I found a brown sweatshirt with a hand-painted leopard on it on sale, and some clunky wooden bead bracelets. I was wearing a pair of tight brown corduroy jeans and they looked great with the new shirt. Then on my way out I threw my trench coat into the rubbish. It really was a mess, a relic from the old Sara Jo look.

All of a sudden it really started to pour. I looked around in a panic (was the leopard going to melt its spots?), and ducked into the health bar next door where I ordered a celery tonic. I drank it standing at the counter, watching a girl grind a bunch of carrots into juice. I was just thinking of buying some high-energy vitamins, when this absolutely fantastic-looking guy bumped into me. He was tan, with streaky blond hair, and he had the most incredible blue eyes. Taffy would have died for him.

"I should say 'excuse me,' " he said, "but I did it on purpose, and I enjoyed it."

"You did?" I didn't know how to handle flirting, and I felt as if I were all legs and no funk. My hair was frizz, and I was sure that my eyes were leaking down my cheeks. He must have been eighteen at least, and definitely a jock.

"I'll buy you another tonic if you sit at a table with me," he said.

I couldn't believe it, but it had happened. I'd finally made it. I was in Taffyville! We sat down at a rickety wooden table and he told me his name was Keith Something-or-other. I wasn't listening, I was too busy looking.

I switched from celery to ginger beer, and Keith ordered a bean sprout, carrot, and raisin salad. There we were, sitting at the same table together. Unbelievable!

"You've got a nice ass," he told me candidly, and I swallowed so hard that the pain brought tears to my eyes. But then I got cool. I could handle it. But I didn't know where

135

to look, and I was afraid if I stared into his eyes or something I'd start to blush. If only I smoked! Then I could fuss around for a while finding a cigarette and lighting it, or do that sexy thing women did — take little bits of tobacco off their tongue with their finger. Instead I moved my glass around on the table, making rings.

"How come I haven't seen you around?" he asked, but he wasn't looking at my face, he was looking right at my boobs, making me think I should start doing some exercises to give nature a push.

"Oh, I'm in and out of town," I said. "In fact, I'm out again tomorrow." I thought I'd better limit this relationship right now, in case he had any ideas. I wasn't sure I was ready for a Keith just yet.

He looked amused. "How old are you?" He was still staring at the same place, and that really made me curious. I mean, Katie was right. I'm small. Did he like that?

"How old do you think?"

"I'm afraid to guess," he said, and then he laughed. Maybe he wasn't very bright. "Okay," Keith said, and slapped some bills down on the table. He pushed his chair back. "My car is outside, I'll give us both a lift."

Now what was I going to do? There wasn't anyplace to go except the bathroom, so that's where I headed. At least I'd have some time to think.

"Be right back." I flashed him a big, bright smile.

"Don't change anything," he said. "I like what I've been seeing."

Past the ladies' room was a short dirty corridor with a screen door at the end of it. I ran down the hall and straight outside and down a back alley to the street. I started to laugh, but my heart was pounding like crazy, too. I kept running until I hit a coffee shop.

It was almost empty, and I sat down in a booth near the back and ordered a lemon Coke. When it came I was starving, so I decided to have a pizza burger and onion rings. And while I was waiting for my food to come, I vowed never to mess with Keith or anyone like him again. L.T. didn't have one damn thing to worry about.

When I got to the movie at seven, the first Chaplin revival had started. I bought some popcorn and settled down to watch. But a few minutes later, the lights came on, and an usher blew a whistle at the back of the theater.

"Is there a Sara Jo Jacoby in the audience, please? Sara Jo Jacoby, please see the manager."

When the lights went off, I jumped up and raced to the back of the theater, imagining all kinds of tragedies. I found the manager's office right away, and opened the door without knocking. There was Daniel. But he didn't look as if anyone had died; he looked angry.

"What are you doing here?" I asked him.

"Well, I looked about everywhere else," he said, shaking his head, and then he thanked the manager, put his hand on my shoulder, and gave me a push.

"Hey —"

"Let's go outside, Sara Jo," he said, and then we were standing in the outer lobby, looking at each other.

"One," Daniel said, "neither Joleen nor I had any idea

where you were. You left the house around two, and Joleen said you casually mentioned something about shopping. She expected you home by five, at the latest."

"Didn't I say that I was going to have something to eat, and then go to the movies?"

"No. You didn't. It's late, and it's getting dark, and we've been very worried."

"I'm sorry," I told him, "honestly."

"Wait a minute, Sara Jo, there's more. You know, you can really be very irresponsible."

"Hey, Daniel, just a min——"

"Mimi is here."

"Oh, shit."

And then Daniel smiled.

"I can't go home," I told him. "I don't want to see her."

"Why not? She's the same person you left in Boston a couple of months ago."

"Maybe. But I'm not the same."

He put his hands on my shoulders. "I guess you're not. But we've still got to get going."

"What's really the problem between you and Mimi, Sara Jo?" Daniel asked when we were in the car. "What's wrong between the two of you?"

"I guess nothing's really wrong," I told him. "I just don't much like her. Is that a terrible thing to say?" I thought about it for a minute, and then I turned to look at him. "You see, Mimi is sort of like this fossil, vegetating around in a house on Beacon Street. She's dusty, and the lace on her dress is crumbling. Do you know what I mean?" I could see the picture perfectly in my head, and Daniel seemed to understand too. He nodded.

Then I wondered what I was talking about anyway. I was right, but so what? I still lived with Mimi. I was still going back to Boston to keep on living with her. I couldn't stay here. So why was I making such a fuss?

We were slowing down to turn into the driveway.

"As soon as we get in the door she's going to say how inconsiderate I am," I told Daniel. "Just wait."

We went through the garage into the dining room where Mimi was sitting at the table with her back to me. Joleen looked very relieved.

"I'm sorry," I said. "I was watching Charlie Chaplin when Daniel finally found me. He had to look all over. I really am sorry."

Mimi didn't turn around, but I knew her eyebrows were peaking up into her hair, and that she was giving Joleen one of her exasperated looks.

"Hello, Aunt Mimi." I walked around and gave her a quick kiss.

"Sara, you behaved very irresponsibly." I shot Daniel a look. "These people will think I've brought you up without any manners. I think you owe everyone an apology."

"I just did apologize," I said. Then I looked at Joleen. "I just forgot."

"You're forgiven. Sit down, Daniel. I've kept something heated for you and Sara Jo."

"Oh, thanks, but I'm not hungry," I told her. "I pigged out on a pizza burger."

"Do you know, Sara Jo, I don't even recognize you." Mimi was inspecting me carefully, and I began to feel uncomfortable.

"How's Thelma?" I asked her.

"Feeling the heat." She pressed her fingers into some crumbs on the tablecloth. "It's those veins of hers. Every summer they give her trouble."

Joleen had just put a plate of roast chicken down in front of Daniel, and he looked relieved to have something to do.

"Poor Thelma. The heat and Heidi too." I was kidding, but I didn't know what else to talk about either. "Is Heidi still having trouble with men?" I asked Mimi, and she frowned at me.

"Sara, I'm sure Joleen and Daniel are not interested in Thelma's domestic problems." She sipped her coffee.

Okay, I wouldn't bait Mimi anymore. It wasn't fair. And in September, I'd be right back in Boston with her. I hated to think about September, because it meant thinking about the crummy school I'd be going to. The one that specialized in graffiti and break dancing. I was sure all the kids there were into heavy metal.

"Will you have another slice of cake, Mimi?" Joleen asked, and just then the door chimes rang.

I jumped up. "I'll go."

L.T.

As soon as I saw him I remembered our one-week anniversary. I would never have forgotten if there hadn't been all that awful stuff over Katie. He had a suit and tie on, and he looked beautiful.

"Oh, L.T.," I wailed.

"Can I come in? What's the matter?"

"Sure, come on in," I gave his hand a quick squeeze. Poor Mimi. I didn't think she was ready for this.

"I forgot," I whispered to him. "I'm sorry."

"You forgot? You forgot that I was coming tonight? That we were supposed to have dinner together? How could you forget that?"

"I'm really sorry, L.T.," I told him again. And I was. But I was also *really* getting tired of saying that I was sorry. When was I going to get to the place where I could do things without apologizing for them?

"And how come you're wearing those jeans?" he asked. "They're too tight."

"Sara Jo?" Daniel called from the dining room.

"Come on," I said to L.T. "The firing squad."

Three faces looked at us from under the dining room chandelier.

"Joleen, Aunt Mimi, this is L.T."

A nod and a smile.

"L.T., this is my aunt, Mimi Jacoby, and this is" — but I couldn't do it; maybe I even wanted to, but I just couldn't — "this is Joleen Wertzburger."

"I guess I forgot everything tonight," I told Daniel, who had been staring at me. "L.T. came over to meet you all, and take me out for dinner."

"For dinner?" Mimi disapproved instantly.

Joleen spoke to L.T. "Sara Jo's aunt is just down from Boston for the night," she explained, "but why don't you both go out to the kitchen? There's angel food cake there, Sara."

"Thank you, Mrs. Wertzburger, and you too, Ms. Jacoby." L.T. was wonderful.

I touched his hand. "This way, L.T."

Once we were alone, I could see that L.T. wasn't sure if he should be angry with me or not.

"Do you forgive me?" I stood on tiptoe to kiss his cheek. Tonight he smelled like pine.

"Yeah, I guess so," he said. "But you'd better get rid of those jeans, Sara Jo. I really mean it." But then he put his arms around me.

"Are you crazy? They could all come piling in here." But I didn't really mind.

"How come your aunt's here?"

"Because she wanted to meet you," I joked. Even if we couldn't go out to dinner, just being with L.T. was great.

"She doesn't look like she should be your aunt," L.T. said, finishing his cake.

"Do you want another piece?"

"Sure."

He was right. Mimi didn't look like my aunt. She didn't *feel* like my aunt. In fact, it was getting harder and harder for me to believe we were even related.

"But you look just like your mother."

"You're crazy, L.T."

"What's the matter with that? Your mother is beautiful, Sara Jo."

"Let's just drop the subject, okay?" I said nervously. I had no intention of trying to explain the complications of Joleen right now. Anyhow, I was getting jumpy about what was

142

happening in the other room. Maybe Mimi was telling Joleen that I should be forbidden to see L.T. — just on general principles, or because I was so irresponsible. I was sure she could think up a reason.

"Should I leave since your aunt is here, Sara Jo?"

I thought about it. "Maybe that would be a good idea," I told him. Even though I hated him to go, I thought if he left it might calm Mimi down. And if I acted like a dutiful niece, maybe she'd keep her mouth closed.

We carried our plates to the sink.

"I'm glad I saw you, even though it wasn't for long," he said.

"I'm glad too, L.T."

We put our arms around each other, and I laid my head against L.T.'s shoulder. We were taking a chance, but I was pretty sure no one would come in.

"L.T., would you kiss me?"

"Are you sure?" he asked pointing to the door behind us.

"Yes." I lifted my head and kissed him with my eyes closed. When I felt his tongue in my mouth, it was like a lick of orange frosting, and that's when I heard the swish of the kitchen door. I pushed L.T. away and swung around, but no one was there.

"Did you hear anyone come in here?" I asked.

"Who?"

"Anyone! I just heard the kitchen door."

"Well, no one's here now," he said logically.

"I know that, L.T."

"So be loose. It was probably your imagination."

I hoped he was right.

143

"Do I look okay?" I asked.

"You look great."

"No, really, L.T."

"Really." He gave me a kiss on the nose.

Once we were in the living room, I felt better because I couldn't find one face that would tell me it had been in the kitchen with L.T. and me.

But after L.T. left, Mimi told me to sit down. She didn't ask, she commanded. Suddenly my face turned warm and pink, and my hands began to shake. My typical reaction to Mimi when she was about to make a pronouncement. But what could she really do to me? Nothing that I couldn't handle now, right? And then I started to get mad. I didn't have to be afraid of Mimi anymore. I wasn't a child. What was she going to do, stop sending my allowance? I started to feel better.

"So." I stretched my legs out in front of me. Very casual. "What's happening? Did everyone like L.T.? I like him a lot."

"So it would appear." Mimi's voice was crackling ice, and Joleen sighed.

"What's the matter, Aunt Mimi?"

"Sara Jo, I was *in* the kitchen with you and your friend."

"You were? I didn't see you." I'd almost forgotten what Mimi's cold blasts were like, but I was remembering pretty quickly.

"You couldn't see me. You were too busy being kissed, and I'll tell you that I didn't expect what I saw."

"We kissed each other, Aunt Mimi. That's all. Just a kiss."

"Sara Jo, your behavior isn't acceptable. That young man —"

"Kissed me," I finished for her. "L.T. only kissed me. And I like him to kiss me, which doesn't exactly put me out there walking the streets, you know!" I was coming unglued.

"I will not listen to another word from you, young lady." Mimi fixed me with her cold turtle eyes.

"Joleen," she said, "I regret this evening very much. And I apologize to you and Daniel. You've had nothing but problems this summer because of my niece."

I could have put a knife through her temple.

"I'm going to take Sara Jo home with me in the morning. This little experiment just isn't working out the way we'd hoped, and—"

"No, Mimi."

I looked at Joleen. She was pale, but she was deadly serious.

"I want Sara Jo here. We'll work out what needs to be done."

"Joleen, I'm sorry, but I'll have to insist. Sara Jo is my responsibility, and—"

"You can't insist, Mimi."

They stared at each other.

"It's legal," Joleen said quietly. "Until September first. I hope this doesn't have to be a battle between us, because I'd be sorry to see that. Very sorry."

I looked at Mimi, but her face was closed.

"I'm going to clear the table," I said, getting up.

Had there really been a lawyer? And had they signed papers about me? Was I *legally* in Locust Valley? The whole thing made me feel like a checker piece.

Joleen came into the kitchen. "Mimi said to say good night, and that she'd be in touch soon."

"The deep freeze," I said.

"I don't think so." Joleen shook her head. "I think she was really upset. You and L.T. seemed to have shocked her."

"I'm going to bed," I said, hoping Joleen wouldn't try to stop me. Luckily, she didn't.

August was hot and humid. The weatherman said that these were the dog days you hear so much about.

Mimi wouldn't even admit that she perspired. She insisted the heat only hurt you when you paid attention to it. We had one small fan that she plugged in about four times a year, and on stifling August nights we occasionally had dinner on the porch, where the jalousies could be opened.

Luckily, Joleen liked the house cold. Some days I wouldn't go outside at all. I'd just lie on my bed, eating fruit and reading. Joleen only occasionally interfered.

"When I was your age, I had lots of boys around," she told me one day.

"Good for you." Since Mimi had left, I'd been very careful about Joleen. I didn't want to give her any reason for coming down heavy on L.T. and me.

"L.T. is very nice, Sara, but —"

"Please don't pick on me, okay?" I'd just finished talking to L.T., and I was in the kitchen getting some cherries.

"We made an agreement, Sara Jo."

"I know the agreement, and I'm sticking to it, aren't I?"

It wasn't an agreement really, it was more of a decision. I could only see L.T. twice a week, and not at night unless we arranged for that specially ahead of time. We were expected to do lots of public things, like visiting museums, and not like sitting in a dark movie, or walking in the woods. So far we'd been to the duck hatcheries and a whaling museum. The whole idea was crazy. It only made L.T. and me hyperaware of what we were supposed to be forgetting.

"I was only pointing out," Joleen said, "that if you paid more attention to other boys —"

"*What* other boys? Am I supposed to hang out on street corners, or spend my time in discos, waiting to be picked up?"

"There's a dance at the veterans' hall tomorrow night. Why don't you go to that?"

"Is that only a suggestion?"

"That's all."

"Then I can't. Tomorrow night, L.T. and I and everybody else in Locust Valley are going to the St. Peter's festival."

"I forgot."

"Excuse me." I picked up my bowl of cherries and got out fast.

L.T. was picking me up at seven-thirty for the carnival, and I had to be in by ten, which gave us two and a half hours together. Skimpy.

To kill time that afternoon I put some silvery polish on my nails and took a long bath in this fantastic stuff Joleen has, called Lactopine. It's a Swiss bath oil, and when you pour it in the tub, the water turns as green as a pine tree. Joleen said she'd get me some before I go back to Boston, but it won't be the same without L.T. saying, "Hey, you smell like Christmas, Sara Jo." I didn't even want to think about what I was going to do without L.T. Yesterday he suggested we run away together, and I wished that we could. Maybe if we got

147

as far as Europe, no one over there would care how old we were. I loved making up fantasies.

We didn't go on many rides at the festival, but we spent a lot of time playing games, including the one where you knock wooden milk bottles down with a softball. I won a money clip shaped like a dollar sign at that one, and I gave it to L.T. He tucked his bills in it and told me he'd keep it forever.

It was only a little after nine when we decided to leave. L.T. had won a transistor radio for me and a giant kangaroo for Lily.

"Do you want to have a pizza?" he asked. We were walking down Main Street with his arm around my waist.

"It's too late," I said unhappily.

"You could call your mother. I bet she wouldn't mind if you were late just every once in a while."

"Ha."

He hugged me closer, "Come on, try."

We were passing a pay phone, and L.T. handed me a quarter.

He was grinning when I came out of the booth. "She said yes, right?"

"Right," I told him, "but I have to be in by eleven." Okay, I thought. So Joleen isn't a monster after all.

Pinza's was small and dark and crowded, but a tiny booth opened up in the back, and L.T. and I squeezed in.

"Are those your knees?" I asked, knocking against him.

He didn't answer, he just took my hand and held it.

When the waiter came we ordered a small Sicilian pie with broccoli on it.

"I have something for you." L.T. reached into his pocket and put a small grey box down in front of me.

"Open it."

I lifted the cover, and then a layer of gauzy cotton.

"Oh, L.T." I held the ring in the palm of my hand. It was a band of silver stars. The most beautiful ring I'd ever seen.

"L.T."

He took it from me and put it on my right hand. "Now don't say anything, Sara Jo. Just listen, okay?"

"Okay."

"I bought this for you because I love you. I'm not going to get serious or anything, I just want you to know."

"I know," I said. "I think I love you too, L.T." I knew it.

"One small Sicilian and two Seven-Ups." The waiter covered our table with plates and the pie, but neither one of us paid any attention to him.

"It's like a friendship ring."

"Oh, I love it so much, L.T." We just kept staring at each other.

"Are you hungry?" he finally asked.

I shook my head.

A little while later, L.T. paid the check, and we walked back to Joleen's, holding hands and fitting together perfectly.

A few doors before home, L.T. stopped and kissed me until my knees got rubbery.

"Are you my girl?" he asked me.

"Yes."

He held me tightly, and I wished that we could both curl up inside each other and stay like that always.

Chapter Twelve

Joleen noticed my ring in the morning, but she didn't make a big deal over it, and that surprised me.

We were in the dining room, waxing and polishing some old oak furniture she'd bought at an auction. It was sweaty work, even with air conditioning.

"Look what L.T. gave me," I said casually after I realized she'd seen the ring.

"Oh, isn't that lovely, Sara." Joleen held my fingers to look at it. "Is it for anything special?"

"L.T. said for friendship."

"That's nice. You know, your father gave me an engagement ring when I was seventeen. He hid it in a box of Cracker Jack."

"He did?" It didn't sound like Harry.

"It was the night of my senior prom, and we'd driven down to the beach to watch it get light. We had a bottle of champagne with us, and a picnic hamper filled with cold chicken and fruit. The Cracker Jack was in the bottom of the hamper.

"I wore that ring on a chain around my neck and inside my clothes for almost two years, until Harry finally wore my father down."

Joleen stopped talking, and I moved to another table leg.

"Does it bother you if I talk like this, Sara Jo?"

"I don't care," I told her, "but the Harry I knew had never seen a box of Cracker Jack."

She stopped talking then, and I was just as glad.

A few days later we went out to buy shoes for Lily, and we decided to have lunch in town.

We ate fried clams at a seafood restaurant overlooking the water. Joleen and I started out by having a nice conversation about Lily. After a while we even discussed Clovis and Katie. But eventually Joleen got back into the past again.

First she told me a lot of Harry stories that I didn't really want to hear, and then she said, "I would have come when he died, but I was afraid it would be too much for you."

I wished I'd missed the whole thing, too.

Harry had been sick at home, and that's where he died of cancer six months later. We had round-the-clock nurses, and I remember the house always smelling of stale flowers and death.

I bought a pair of earplugs because I could hear Harry moaning at night, and that used to terrify me. Mimi found out about them one night when they thought he was dying. She came in to wake me, and I didn't hear her. So she took the plugs away from me because she said I had to face reality. Luckily I had to face it for only one more week.

The night Harry really did die, Mimi came in for me again. She'd been crying, and her mouth and cheeks were all puffed up.

I stood outside the door of his room and, when I didn't move, Mimi pushed me inside.

Harry was so small; he looked dead already. His eyes were closed, and I closed mine too because I didn't want to look at him. And then he started shouting. I opened my eyes, and he was looking at me as if he wanted to kill me. Finally, Mimi pressed my shoulder and turned me toward the door, and that was when Harry called me a whore. He said I was just like my mother, and he kept repeating "whore" over and over again, until Mimi grabbed my hand and pulled me out of the room.

She kept whispering to me that Harry hadn't meant it, that he didn't know what he was saying. But he did mean it, and I knew that.

"Sara Jo? Did you love your father?" Joleen made me jump.

"Right before Harry died," I said, "he told me I was a whore, just like you."

Joleen's eyes got small and angry. She looked just like me.

"Yes, he used to say that to me sometimes, when I was drinking. He thought I was unfaithful to him."

"Were you?"

"No, Sara Jo. Not ever."

She took a sip of coffee.

"I used to come home late, and once I even stayed out all

night. The birds and I woke up on Boston Common. I was pretty scraggly when I got home that morning, but I was alone."

I held my breath and dove. "How come you drank like that?" I asked her. "It made you sick, didn't it? I can remember that, and you and Harry, you used to fight all the time too."

Joleen pushed a saltshaker around on the table. "It did make me sick," she said, without looking up. "I hated it."

"I don't understand."

She sighed, and then she looked straight at me. "It's so hard to make it all short and understandable for you," she said, "and it's hard to go back there and remember too, because it still hurts."

"It's okay," I told her quickly, "you don't have to."

She gave me a crooked smile. "I do have to make a little bit of a beginning, though, don't I?" She reached out and touched my hand and her fingers were very cold. "I don't want to give you too much at once, Sassy." And then she shook her head. "You're not so sassy anymore, are you?"

All at once, that name didn't sound so terrible to me. I remembered that Joleen used to use it teasingly, when she'd give me a quick hug for no reason at all.

"Anyhow," she went on, "I guess the simplest way to put it is that I drank because I felt like such a failure. With Harry, with Mimi and all her standards, and even with the house. That place got to be like a great big monster to me — the old family home where there always seemed to be dust gathering in some corner or other, and newspapers, junk

153

where it shouldn't be. I was young, and I was immature in a lot of ways too. Mostly, I just wanted to play house and be with Harry. But he expected a lot more of me. He thought I could run things — the house, the meals, all of it — but I couldn't. The truth is, I probably didn't even try that hard.

"Harry said very little, but after we'd been married less than a year I sensed his disapproval in the silences that got longer and longer between us. The way he'd kind of remove himself from me, as if we weren't even sitting there in the same room together."

I nodded, because I knew just what she meant.

"Mimi meant well, I guess, but she just made everything worse. She knew what Harry wanted — the way he liked things to be — and she just did everything right for him. She'd try to show me, to explain, but it got so that I despaired of ever coping, and she got very impatient with me. Eventually," Joleen grinned, "I got angry. What did it matter if there were a few ruffled rugs or smudgy windows? When Harry came home from work I only wanted to sit down and talk to him, and listen to what he had to say. I wanted us to share things together, but that never seemed to happen. I guess he wanted a full-time wife, and I only thought about having a playmate I loved, to have fun with.

"He read his paper, or he watched the news, and then on the dot of seven he had to have his dinner. Everything was so organized, every day seemed to have slots where all the right things had to be fitted in. There was no room for us to be young and silly together."

"Is it because he was so much older than you were?" I

asked her, thinking of the ten years that separated their ages, but Joleen shook her head quickly.

"No, I think most of it was that *I* was so young — emotionally, I mean. And there were other problems. . . . But then, pretty quickly, I discovered that a glass or two of wine before Harry came home did a lot to relax me. Naturally for me a glass or two turned into a lot more than that, and pretty soon I stopped trying to make things work, not that I'd actually tried very hard before that. I left everything up to Mimi. I didn't care anymore, except" — she reached across to squeeze my hand — "about you. I never stopped caring about you for a minute, Sara Jo, but I don't know if that's something you can believe yet or not."

I wanted to. I wanted to so badly, but I wasn't sure how I felt either.

And then I did something without thinking about it. I told Joleen about how much I'd missed her and how badly I hurt. I told her about searching for pictures of her, something to see and remember. And then I talked about the letters I'd written to her. I told her all about them.

When I finished, Joleen was teary. "What happened to those letters?" she asked me.

"I threw them out. One day I just got rid of them. I guess that was when I tried to make myself stop thinking about you. I knew you'd never come back."

We sat without speaking for a long while. The waitress had cleared the table long ago, and we left when it was time for dinner, still with the quiet between us, as if neither one of us was ready yet to touch what we'd shared.

Later that night Joleen came in to ask me if I wanted to watch Johnny Carson with her. Daniel was away at a medical convention.

We watched the TV in their room with pillows piled behind us on the bed.

"It took me a long time to realize that Harry had some problems of his own." Joleen picked up the threads as though we'd only paused in between. "He was a perfectionist, he was compulsive about everything, and soon enough I think we both knew I wasn't the kind of wife he wanted or needed. I was pregnant with you when I tried to talk to Mimi about it. I told her how cold and unkind Harry could be, how I wasn't sure he loved me anymore, but she said it was just my nerves, because I was pregnant. She said I needed to make more of an effort and do the right things for Harry. In a way she was right because I was very immature. But she was wrong, too. Harry and I were not meant to be together."

Joleen sighed and shook her head. "Mimi would never believe that her brother could be less than perfect. She blamed everything on all the pressures he had at work. Sara Jo, she lived with us! She heard the fights, and —" Joleen broke off. "I'm sorry, Sara Jo. I really am. You don't need to hear this kind of history."

"It's all right," I told her. But it wasn't. I didn't want to hear any more. All my life no one ever told me anything, and then, in one day — zapperoonie! It was suddenly too much and it was happening too quickly. I was checking out.

I yawned, stretched, and stood up. "I'm exhausted," I said to Joleen. "Good night."

"I'm sorry, honey, I didn't mean to rush everything at you.

156

Sleep well." She looked like she wanted to say something else, but I was grateful that she didn't.

L.T. was the only person I felt close to now. Except for Katie, and I couldn't see her. Why did Joleen tell me all those things? And why didn't she explain why she left *me*? Not Harry, me.

Over the weekend Locust Valley was having a big Americana fair on the high school grounds, and I planned to spend a lot of time there.

First there was a parade through town with floats, a band, and even some trained dogs, who wore ruffles around their necks and did somersaults.

The last float was in the bed of a truck decorated with red, white, and blue bunting, and "America the Beautiful" was piped through a loudspeaker mounted on top. This was the finale, and in the center of the float sat Betsy Ross, dressed in a hoop skirt and a navy jacket painted with silver stars. She was sewing a huge American flag.

Everyone cheered as Betsy hammed it up, bowing and waving, and every so often she'd salute the crowd, or show us the V for victory sign.

When the truck got close to me, I realized it was Katie, her dark braids turned into bunches of curls peeking out from a bonnet that was tied under her chin.

We were both still for a moment as we looked at each other. Then the music picked up, and I thought Katie gave me a special salute as the truck passed.

I followed the crowd to the fairgrounds where I bought a

cornhusk doll dressed in a lace shawl for Lily. I met Katie when I got in line for the Yankee pot roast dinner. All the meat, noodles, and red cabbage you could eat for a dollar fifty. Katie was right in front of me, and she had a heaped plate, plus apple pie and milk.

"You want to eat with me, Betsy?" I asked her. "You look terrific." It was so great to see her again.

She grinned, but I knew she was nervous. We found a table and sat down, and then we got lucky. Clovis appeared out of the crowd with a mug of coffee in her hand. She stood over us and beamed. "How nice!" she said. "How really nice. And I'm not going to interrupt a thing. I just came over to say hi, hi." And then she was gone, as if she'd been a strange illusion.

"Hey, Katie, am I being welcomed back into the family?"

"Beats me," she said, and the two of us started to giggle.

"So, how's L.T.?" she asked.

And then Katie and I were back together again. We talked about everything but being quarantined from each other. She didn't bring it up, and I didn't want to either. I felt terrific. After a half hour, it might as well not have happened anyway. Katie and I were solid.

"Hey, you want to do something morbid with me tomorrow?" she asked.

"Morbid? What's morbid?"

Katie giggled. "Clovis stuck me in this Vacation Bible School, and there's a kid in my class who says 'morbid' about practically everything. Like last week, the teacher asked Rollo, that's his name, she asked him to describe Jesus' childhood. So Rollo says, 'It was really morbid.' Don't you think that's funny, Sara Jo?"

"Not bad," I said. "What do you want to do tomorrow?"

"Maybe we could go to the beach. Do you want to? We could take the bus to Captree. Rollo says it's the best A-number-one beach on Long Island."

Rollo again, huh?

We decided that I'd make fried chicken wings and Katie would do marshmallow fudge and lime Kool-Aid, and that would be it. Katie called it a no-frills picnic.

Unfortunately Taffy came to the beach with us.

"I need to swim for hours," she said, patting her flat stomach. "I gained two pounds."

"How utterly, utterly awful," Katie mocked.

Then Taffy zeroed in on me. She looked me up and down as if I were a dummy in a store window, but luckily I was pretty far beyond the place where Taffy could intimidate me. I just let her stare.

"You look pretty good, Sara Jo," she said, sounding a little surprised, and then she sniffed appreciatively. "What's that perfume you're wearing?"

"She uses toilet water, right out of the john. It's very morbid," Katie said, breaking herself up. There was something about being with Taffy that brought out everything childish in Katie, but I didn't mind. I was just glad to be with her again.

It was late when we got to the beach, and a lot of people

were leaving so we had yards of empty sand to ourselves.

"Rollo lent me his metal detector," Katie said, opening a collapsible rod. "It's really morbid."

"Who's Rollo?" Taffy asked without much curiosity, and then, as she looked at the metal detector, "and what's morbid about it?"

Katie giggled.

"Rollo is morbid," I said, "right, Katie?"

"Is he cute?" Taffy wanted to know.

The rod had a silver disk at the end of it, and Katie was passing it along the top of the sand.

"How do I know? Is that the only thing you can think about? How someone looks?" Katie sounded disgusted. She jammed the metal detector into the sand, sat down next to it, and looked straight at Taffy. "Rollo has a space between his two front teeth that he can whistle through, and he has freckles on his nose, just like Sara Jo, and he wants to be a mineralogist. Okay? Are you satisfied now?"

Taffy raised her eyebrows and shrugged. "He sounds like a winner," she said. "I'm going to swim. Anyone want to come?"

"Not me," Katie and I said together, and Taffy took off for the water.

"Alone at last," I sighed. "Why did she have to come with us? You'd have to spend a week trying to explain to her what a mineralogist is. I don't know what any guy would see in her, except for her face and her bod."

Katie looked embarrassed. "I think my mother thought we should have some company along."

"Oh no," I groaned, "she thinks I'm going to torture you again."

"Sara Jo —"

"No, Katie, wait, I want to say something," I interrupted her.

But then she said, "I just wanted to tell you that you didn't torture me." Katie ducked her head and fiddled around in the sand as if she were looking for shells. "I was a jerk."

"No you weren't," I said firmly, "I was. I insist on being the prime jerk."

That made us both laugh and without saying anything about it we made an agreement not to talk about the weeks we hadn't seen each other.

"Tell me about L.T. Really, Sara Jo, I want to hear. Honest."

I believed her, but I didn't want to talk to anyone about L.T. and me right now. He was kind of private, like this treasure I had that I could take out whenever I wanted to, when I was alone, and just savor it all by myself. Someday I'd probably share him with Katie, but not just yet.

"I still see him," I told her. "I really like him a lot." The understatement of the year, but Katie didn't push me.

"Now you tell me about Rollo," I said, but I was careful not to tease her.

"He's great!" Katie's eyes lit up. "He knows about all kinds of terrific stuff, like rocks and stars — just stuff, you know?" She started digging tunnels in the sand with her heels. "It's no great big romance or anything," she assured me.

"Of course not," I told her solemnly.

Katie jumped up. "You want to make a sand castle? You want to make the greatest, biggest, most humongous sand castle —" and then she stopped.

"What's the matter?"

"I don't know . . ." She made a face. "Do you think that's kid stuff or something?"

"Are you crazy? I love sand castles." I really did.

For the rest of the afternoon we worked away like twin architects, constructing a sand city with canals and moats and loads of dripping towers in varying heights. Taffy looked at us as if she thought we belonged in nursery school, but that was fine with Katie and me, because she left us alone and it gave us time to catch up with each other and trade stories.

It was a wonderful day, and on the way home Katie and I sang all the verses to "One Hundred Bottles of Beer on the Wall," while Taffy moved to the back of the bus and pretended not to be with us.

That night I went to bed at eight o'clock. I was very sleepy from the beach, but by eleven I was wide awake again so I decided to go downstairs and read.

The hall upstairs was quiet, as if everyone had been asleep for hours. Lily's door was open, and I peeked in. She had a junior bed with the sides pulled up, and the cornhusk doll was propped in one corner. Lily was sleeping in a pair of pants with the Three Little Pigs running around on them. I wanted to pick her up and cuddle her, but I knew she'd have me for a few stories, a glass of milk, and maybe even a jelly sandwich.

We're partly family, I thought, looking down at her small round shoulders and the damp curls near her ear. Lily is my half sister, and maybe she'll find me again when she grows up, or I'll find her. Or I could even write to her from Boston, so she won't have a chance to forget about me.

This was only a visit, I thought, holding onto the side of Lily's bed; I don't belong here. Before I knew it, I was crying, and there was such a hard knot in my throat that it was difficult to swallow.

What's the matter with you? I asked myself. Do you actually want to stay here?

The living room was dark, but a light was coming from the dining room, and I could hear Joleen's voice. She was on the phone.

"No, Mimi, things are much quieter now," I heard her say, and then I stopped to listen.

"Yes, I know September is getting closer. It's going to be very strange — well, it's going to be a lot more than that, for all of us, not to have Sara Jo here anymore. . . ."

I couldn't stand it another minute. Tears were pouring down my face, and I ran upstairs, making little gulping sounds, and trying not to cry out loud.

I'm not even a person anymore, I thought, jumping into bed and huddling under the covers. I'm this *object* that gets picked up there and then put down here. And now I'm going to get picked up and dumped again!

I heard Joleen come upstairs, then the soft click of their bedroom door. The house was silent, and I finally stopped crying. I turned over on my back and stared at the ceiling, waiting for it to get light. I knew I couldn't face anyone tomorrow. Not Daniel and not Lily, and certainly not Joleen. I'd gotten a mother lent to me for three months, and now I was going to be abandoned again. No! I just wouldn't let it happen that way. This time I would be the one to go. I'd leave first.

Chapter Thirteen

By six-thirty, before anyone was up, I was out of the house and halfway to Locust Valley. There was a ground fog, and that made me feel safe. I'd stuffed a pair of khaki shorts and a couple of shirts in a tote bag, and I had the "emergency" money that Mimi had told me to use only under the most dire circumstances, although she knew, of course, that such circumstances would never arise. Ha. As usual, Mimi didn't know anything.

There was a bus terminal in town, and my plan was to hang out there until after nine so I could call L.T. after Hank had left for work. I knew his parents were away on vacation.

It was a long wait, and when I finally heard his voice on the phone it was still cloudy with sleep.

"Hi, L.T." I leaned my head against the wall of the booth and started to cry again.

"Is that you, Sara Jo?"

"Yes."

"What's the matter? You sound like you're crying."

"L.T., I'm at the bus station. Could you — do you want to come here and meet me?"

"Sure, just give me ten minutes to get dressed. Sara Jo? Are you going somewhere? What are you doing?"

"I don't know, L.T. I just have to get away. I have to leave."

While I was waiting for him to come I bought a one-way ticket to New York City, and then I went back and bought another one. I didn't have to ask, I just knew L.T. would want to come with me.

He was panting when he came through the glass doors of the bus station, and his shirttail was hanging out, but I was so glad he was there that I ran up and gave him a hug.

"What's happening?" he said, holding onto my shoulders. I knew one of us was shaking. Maybe we both were.

"I have to get out of here, L.T. Could you just trust that?"

"Are you running away?"

I held up one bus ticket and showed it to him.

"No way," he said, reaching for his wallet. "I'm getting one too. I'm going with you."

I held up the other ticket and tried to grin.

"You promise not to ask me a lot of questions?" I said to him while we waited for the bus.

"I'll promise to try not to." He gave me a quick hug around the shoulders, but he looked worried.

At the bus terminal in New York we found a crowded coffee shop with steamy windows. After waiting for fifteen minutes we got a table, but when we sat down there was a mess of dirty dishes between us. I looked down at a cigarette butt floating at the bottom of a coffee cup, and I had to fight not to cry.

"L.T., I can't go into everything now. There are so many things to explain, and they all hurt too much. But I — just — I don't belong anywhere — not here, and not in Boston —"

"As far as I'm concerned you belong right here," L.T. said firmly, banging his hand on the table and making the silverware jump.

A waitress collected the dirty dishes and slapped a wet rag around on some coffee rings.

"Where do you want to go, Sara?" he asked, touching the back of my hand.

"I don't know," I said miserably. "I can't seem to think of anything. I have some money, but — how old do you think I look, L.T.?"

He grinned at me. "When you cry, you look like you're about nine years old, Sara Jo. Maybe even eight."

"That's not funny! I'm trying to be serious because I have to make some plans."

"Okay, don't get mad. I want to help you, honest." He ran his fingers through his hair, making the cowlicks stand up in little spikes on the back of his head. Then he looked at me for a long time, considering. "I don't know," he said finally, "how old do you want to look?"

"Old enough to get a job — maybe?" I didn't have much hope, but the situation was desperate. I had to think up some plan.

L.T. looked unhappy. He shook his head and stared down at the plate of bacon and eggs that the waitress had just put in front of him.

"Not that old, Sara Jo. Not even when you get dressed up. Besides, what do you want to get a job for? In this city? It would be much too dangerous. I'd never let you do that." He broke his egg up into little pieces, but he didn't eat anything.

I wasn't hungry either.

"I know. It probably wasn't a very good idea. I just can't seem to think of what to do. You know what, L.T.? I hate everything. I really do. Every damn thing."

"Except me?"

"Absolutely except you." What would I do without L.T.? He leaned across the table and kissed me on the nose.

"Maybe we should go to a movie?" I said. "Maybe I'll be able to think better in the dark."

When we got up to leave, L.T. put his arm around me. "I can feel you trembling," he said.

I hid my face against his shoulder. It felt warm and safe being next to him, and I wanted to go on feeling like that forever.

"I could hold you all day, Sara, but we'd probably get arrested or something." He gave me a little push, and we walked out into the hot, sticky street together.

By that evening we were both exhausted. We had seen five movies and both of us were feeling bloated and sick from popcorn and cheese nachos. In the dark theaters I just leaned against L.T.'s shoulder, or we held hands. I couldn't come up with any plan. In fact, I didn't seem able to think at all. Either I watched the screen for a while, or I thought how nice it was to be close to L.T. To look up and see his profile in the dark.

By eleven o'clock that night we were standing in front of the Port Authority bus terminal again, and I was getting more and more anxious. I started to cry.

"I don't know how you can stand me," I said to L.T. "I can't stand myself! I'm such a pain."

"I could stand you anytime, Sara Jo. Honest, I don't care how you act. But its late, and your mom is going to be really worried." He put his arm around me. "Come on, let's go home, all right?"

"No!" I pulled away from him. "I can't go back there! You're just going to have to believe me, L.T. I can't."

"Then what are we going to do?" He was beginning to sound pretty desperate himself. "I don't think I could stand to see one more movie, Sara Jo. Not even for you."

"I know." And then a thought finally come to me. "I know what I'll do," I said. "It's the only thing I can do. I'm going to go to Boston. After all, I have to go back there eventually, so I might as well get it over with. That's it, L.T., I'll take the next bus up to Boston." That's where I lived, wasn't it? With Mimi. But I wished that everything were different. I wished that so hard. I hated the idea of Boston, but even more than that I hated knowing it wouldn't be difficult for Joleen to let me go back there, not after the way I'd behaved all summer. Like a barbed wire fence, poking her whenever she tried to get close to me.

"If you really want to go to Boston, then I'm coming with you," L.T. said, and even though I knew that was a crazy idea and that Mimi would probably have a fit, I didn't say anything to stop him. I wanted him to be there with me, on that long bus trip.

But after my big decision, it turned out that we were out of luck anyway. Or at least we were until seven-thirty the next morning. That's when the next bus left for Boston.

"If we're going to have to spend the night here, I'd better get myself a razor for the morning," L.T. said, rubbing his hand over his chin.

I looked at him and grinned, giving him a shove. "Come on, who are you kidding, L.T.? You don't shave yet."

"Darn right I do," he said, sounding like I'd hurt him. "Here, feel." He rubbed his cheek up and down against mine. I could feel little bristles scrape my face, and that seemed the most intimate moment L.T. and I had ever shared.

That night I fell asleep on a hard bench with my head in his lap. It was hot and uncomfortable, but I was so tired that I slept anyhow, feeling as if I never wanted to wake up again in my whole entire life.

The next morning we went back to the same coffee shop to have breakfast before the bus left. L.T. had shaved in the men's room and there was a little knick on his chin that I kept wanting to touch. Knowing that he shaved made him seem older to me. He was hungry when we sat down, but I didn't even want to think about food. My stomach was flipping around too much.

"I'll just have water," I told the waitress.

"Dollar minimum at the table," she said, looking bored.

"That's okay," L.T. said. "Maybe she'll want something to eat later."

"Suit yourselves."

I pushed a fly off the sugar shaker, and L.T. took my hand.

"What's the matter, Sara Jo? You look so unhappy."

I shook my head, because I was afraid that if I tried to explain, to say anything at all, the tears would start all over again.

"You're afraid, aren't you?" L.T. guessed.

"Yes. But it's more than that. L.T., I'm so mixed up." My throat felt swollen. But it wasn't just fear, I knew that. Something was slipping away from me, and I wanted it back.

"We'll be together. That will make it easier, won't it?" L.T. was trying so hard that I really had to keep swallowing so that I wouldn't cry.

When his breakfast came, I broke off a piece of bacon.

"Great! You're eating," he said, grinning, "Do you want a plate for yourself?"

"No, it's more fun this way." I was beginning to feel a little better because the two of us were together, which meant nothing could be that bad. Not really.

"L.T., I think maybe I'm getting hungry."

"Here comes the waitress. Order something, Sara Jo. It might make you feel better if you eat."

"Thank you, sir. I will obey."

I ordered ham and sausages and pancakes, and while I was eating, ravenously, I made a decision that made me feel better than I had since before I left Locust Valley.

"L.T.?" I traced a circle around his knuckle with my finger. I loved his hands.

"What?"

"I think I have to go back to Locust Valley. No, I don't *think* it, I know it. I can't go to Boston without going there first. I want to see Joleen, my — my — mother, and I want to tell her good-bye, and that I'm sorry —" But I couldn't finish explaining to L.T., because I knew if I did I'd start to cry and I wouldn't be able to stop.

L.T. came around the table and gave me a big hug and a kiss. "That's great, Sara Jo," he said, and I thought he really looked relieved.

"I'm going in with you," L.T. said when we got to the house, and he held my hand as we walked up the path. Then the front door flew open and Joleen came running toward us. She looked happy, but she didn't hug me.

"I'm so glad —"

"I'm so sorry I —"

We both started to laugh.

"L.T. wants —"

"Mrs. Wertzburger —"

And then the three of us started laughing. I guess we were all pretty nervous.

"Come inside, you two," Joleen said. "There's been a lot of commotion here."

As I stepped into the foyer, Lily hurled herself into me. "Never leave Lily! She kill you!"

I picked her up in my arms and kissed her. "I missed you, princess. I missed you, missed you, missed you!"

And then I saw Mimi. She was sitting up straight in a chair, and looking as if I'd already been disowned.

"Hello, Aunt Mimi." I just couldn't make myself go over and kiss her.

"Hello, Ms. Jacoby."

She didn't answer either of us, and I was relieved when Joleen came in and sat down.

I turned and looked at her. "I ran away," I said, "or I wanted to, and L.T. came with me because I called him."

"Why?" Her voice was low, almost gentle. And for once I didn't want to make fun of her, or tell her she could go to hell, either.

"I knew I didn't want to leave here," I said, looking down at the rug, frightened. "I ruined everything — the whole summer —"

"Well, I'm glad you realize that." Mimi turned to me, and her face was lobster red.

"Aunt Mimi, I'm try to ex——"

"Where were you? Both of you? And what were you doing? That's what I'd like to hear. Oh, this is too much, Sara Jo, it really is."

"We only went to New York," L.T. explained, "that's all."

"For the night?" Aunt Mimi was in a rage.

"Ms. Jacoby? May I say something?" L.T. was standing up. "I want to say this to you too, Mrs. Wertzburger." He looked at Joleen. "I like Sara Jo very much, but I respect her too. We spent last night sitting up in the Port Authority bus terminal, in the city. That's where we were."

Just then Lily jumped up from the floor where she'd been sitting, and ran over to kick L.T. in the leg as hard as she could. "Sarry love Lily!" she told him while L.T. rubbed his leg.

Joleen grabbed Lily, plunked her down between us on the

couch, and gave her foot a sharp slap. "I'm sorry," she told L.T. "No. *She's* sorry, aren't you, brat?" But Lily wouldn't answer.

L.T. was blushing, and I thought his courage had deserted him. I got up and took his hand, and we stood there looking at each other for a moment. And then something quiet and warm settled inside me. I felt as if I were coming to a stop for the first time this summer. I didn't have to be afraid of Mimi, or hide letters in shoe boxes, or do anything crazy like getting drunk. And I didn't have to hate Joleen. I loved her, and everything felt soft and comfortable for the first time that I could remember.

I didn't hear what else L.T. said, but I knew he'd done it just right from the look on Joleen's face. Mimi was staring at him as if he were a liar, but the hell with Mimi.

L.T. smiled at me. "I think I'd better get home and let my parents chew me out a little bit."

I walked him to the door, and in the foyer I kissed him softly on the lips. "You're wonderful," I said.

"He's a winner, Sara Jo," Joleen told me when I came back into the living room.

"Yeah, he sure is," I said.

"Sara Jo, I've been here since last night," Mimi said. "And I have something to tell you before I take the plane back this evening." I was really surprised that she'd flown down. Mimi has never trusted airplanes. They're too modern for her.

It was still very hard for me to believe that I was going back to Boston next week, but at least I had a few days left here. I really wanted that. The house in Boston — I could practically feel it falling down on me. My room with its ballet dancers doing arabesques along the walls, and all my little-girl furniture with flounces and ruffles on everything. I thought about the poster of Elvis, really dishing it, that I'd tacked defiantly to my bathroom door. Mimi thought he was a degenerate.

"I'm afraid that I just can't take any more strain from you, Sara Jo."

"What do you mean, Aunt Mimi?" My heart had begun to beat like crazy, and I was sweating.

Joleen put her hand on mine for a moment.

"I mean that I am no longer able to act as your guardian. I've never really understood you, Sara, and the older you get the less able I am to cope with what Joleen says is simply your growing up. I can't handle your lack of respect and total disregard for anyone but yourself any longer," she finished, white in the face and shaky.

It wasn't until Joleen handed me some tissues that I realized I was crying. It wasn't that I even wanted to have Mimi be my "guardian" or anything, but being rejected by her like that hurt anyway.

"But you're exceedingly lucky," Mimi continued. "Joleen has volunteered to be legally responsible for you. Frankly, Sara Jo, I don't know why she made the offer. From what I've seen and heard, you've been nothing but a heartache to her all summer long."

"Mimi, that's not true, and you know nothing of my feelings, so don't try to voice them for me," Joleen said crisply.

"I'll have all the necessary papers drawn up, of course," Mimi said, "and —"

"You mean you just plan to give me away? Like something

you don't want? Like a thing going to a rummage sale? I get on your nerves, so you're disposing of me?" What was I? A piece of merchandise to be traded back and forth?

"Sara Jo, you're being ridiculously melodramatic," Mimi said.

I wanted to spit at her, or hit her, or do something. My face was so hot. God, I hated Mimi, I hated her so much.

Joleen reached across Lily and took my hand. She was so cool, and I was burning.

"Sara Jo? This summer, you were right here with me all the time, but I kept missing you, probably because I wanted so badly to 'have' you. Only you kept dodging me, so I tried harder and I made mistakes. I suppose we both did. Maybe now we'll have some time to look for each other. I hope we will, honey."

I knew Joleen had just given me something, but I was confused, and too angry about Mimi to do anything with it.

"Joleen, I believe it's time for me to leave for the airport," Mimi said.

"Sara Jo, I will expect to see and hear from you from time to time." She would?

Mimi collected her handbag and gloves, and tugged at the jacket of her suit. "I'll be in touch," she said, and then she left.

While Joleen and Lily drove Mimi to the airport, I took a shower, and then I called Katie to ask her if I could use the pool. I didn't want to have to think.

"Yeah, sure." She sounded excited.

"Great. Listen, I'll —"

"Sara Jo, wait till I tell you! You're really gonna die! Are you ready?"

"Shoot," I told her.

"No more Delaneys!" Katie sang into the phone.

"You're kidding! How come?" I felt glad just to be talking to her.

"My mother decided they were making me too neurotic. Isn't that wizard?"

Wizard. I guessed that Rollo had a whole vocabulary of his own.

"That means you don't have to wear the sunflower anymore!"

"I'll be right over."

Katie was wearing a snorkeling mask and tube, and when she saw me she jumped up from the side of the pool and pointed under the water.

"You see those flippers?" she asked. "That's Rollo. He's looking for bugs."

"There are *bugs* in the pool?"

"He put them in for us to catch. There must be three hundred of them floating around under there."

Terrific. I could hardly wait to dive in.

Katie pulled at a rubber foot that had surfaced.

"Hey, Rollo, it's Sara Jo!"

"Leave him alone," I told her. "I'm not a celebrity."

"No way. He really wants to meet you."

Rollo surfaced and pulled off his goggles. I looked at his hands, but there were no bugs crawling around on them.

"Hi," I smiled at him.

"How do you do?" He swam to the side of the pool to shake hands with me.

Katie had forgotten to say that he had platinum hair and an English accent.

The three of us played water ball for a while, and then Rollo let me use his snorkling stuff so that Katie and I could hunt June bugs.

Later, when we were sitting on the grass talking, Katie gave me a tweak on the knee. "Sara Jo, how long are you going to stay? I think you should stay forever, and not go back there. Locust Valley has a keen senior high school. You can ask Rollo's brother, he goes there. Right, Rollo?"

"My brother, Cary, would be happy to meet you and tell you about school, Sara Jo." Rollo sounded so formal. He was really cute.

"Oh, boy, you should just see Cary once, Sara Jo. You'd never look at L.T. again!"

"Katie!"

"What's the matter?" She looked innocent.

"You talk too much is what's the matter."

"If you'd give me your number, Sara Jo?" Rollo asked me.

I looked at both of them. "If I do go to school here, I'm sure your brother and I will meet each other." Then I looked at Katie. "And you've never even seen L.T."

Just then Clovis called out that Joleen wanted me for dinner. I hated to leave, because everything was so uncomplicated here with Katie and Rollo.

When I came through the back door, Joleen was cutting tomatoes, Lily was chopping up the floor with her rubber tomahawk, and Daniel was squeezing ice cubes into a pitcher. I stood at the door watching them, and little chills chased up my arms. They were a family, all right. But were they *my* family?

Daniel noticed me first, and he came over and hugged me.

"I'm all wet," I said.

"I don't mind." He hugged me again, and it was shivery inside his arms.

After dinner he went back to the hospital, and Joleen and I cleaned up the kitchen.

"There's only ten days until school begins," Joleen said.

"I know." I put potato salad in a Tupperware bowl and burped it neatly.

Joleen grinned. "I can't do that." She was wrapping pork chops in foil. "Daniel and I came up with two choices for you, Sara. Temporary choices at least, since we're so pressed for time. First, there's a senior high in town —"

"I know."

"Well, there's also a girls' academy in Glen Cove, which isn't far away. You could be a day student there, or you could board, and then spend weekends with us if you wanted to," she said.

I didn't have an answer, so I scoured the sink and cleaned all the countertops. Finally, when there was nothing left to do, I hung up the dish towel and followed Joleen into the living room.

I was nervous because I wanted to ask her something important. I sat down on a hassock and looked into the empty fireplace.

"I want to ask you a question," I said to Joleen, "okay?"

"Anything you want, Sara Jo."

"I know why you left Harry," I said nervously, "but I don't know why you left me." I said that part quickly, like I couldn't wait to get the words out of my mouth. I didn't look at Joleen.

"Oh, Sara. There are so many answers to that question, and none of them are simple. Someday, not a crazy, mixed-up day like today, but someday very soon, I'll explain so many things to you. What it comes down to, honey, just to say it simply, is that I was a drunk. I couldn't even take care of myself, and I did a lot of irresponsible things, but leaving you was the very worst thing I've ever done."

I sat silently for a while. All of a sudden I was totally exhausted.

I got up. "All right," I said, "I'm going to go to bed now."

"That's a good idea," Joleen said. "Sleep well, honey."

The next morning Lily attacked me at seven-thirty with a cold pancake she'd carried up from the kitchen.

"Here, Sara," she said. So it was finally Sara. I smiled sleepily.

The pancake was rolled up, and she carefully spread it out on her palm. Then she bent down for a glass jug that had maple syrup in it. So far she was balancing everything perfectly.

I closed my eyes, and when I opened them, Lily had poured syrup on the pancake, her feet, and the rug.

"That's beautiful, Lily."

"Here." She lifted the soggy mess to my mouth, and I took a bite.

"Did you make this?"

She nodded seriously.

"It's delicious," I said, and gave her some.

After we'd finished the pancake, I put on a pair of old jeans and we went downstairs.

Joleen and Daniel were still having breakfast, so I poured myself a glass of milk and sat down with them. Lily climbed on Daniel's lap and helped herself to some of his scrambled egg.

"She's getting to be some cook," I told Joleen.

"How did you like the syrup?"

"That was the best part."

"Sara Jo, I'd like to be able to tell you we're not trying to rush you about school," Daniel said, taking a sip of his coffee.

"But you are rushing me, right?" I looked at both of them. "It's all right. I know what to do. I think I do anyhow. I'd like to go to the school in town, and live here — with all of you." I thought about the bedroom upstairs. That was mine now, maybe not junior deb's, but mine. I belonged there.

"You live here with Lily, Sara! You live here, or Lily make you dead!"

"Well, that's clear enough." Joleen laughed.

"You win!" I told her. "I'll live here with Lily."

Daniel put Lily down and came over to give me a kiss on the cheek.

"I feel good," I said, looking around the table. "A little weird, maybe, but good."

Joleen grinned. "Sassy Jo was always a little bit weird," she said.

*

Later that afternoon I called L.T., and we made plans to go strawberry picking in some fields outside of town. A lot of rules had been suspended until school started.

"L.T., I don't think this is the heart of the strawberry season on Long Island," I told him, picking around the leaves for any stray pieces of fruit the birds had missed.

"You'd better watch it when we're in school, Sara Jo," he said, out of nowhere.

"Why?"

"Too many boys around."

"Hundreds," I said. "Wow, I can play the field!"

"Hey!" L.T. dropped the half empty basket, and we stopped walking.

"You wouldn't mess around with anyone else, would you?" L.T. looked so upset, I couldn't stand it.

"Never. I couldn't be with anyone but you, L.T."

"I think we're going to get married someday, Sara Jo," he told me solemnly.

"What day?" I asked him, taking his hand.

"In five years," he said, as if he'd thought it all out and come to a definite conclusion. "You'll be eighteen, and I'll have graduated from MIT."

Then we stopped and looked at each other. "We're being crazy," I told L.T.

"That's all right." He held me in his arms, and then he kissed me.

"I love you," we said to each other, and then we turned with our hands holding tight and started the long walk home.